Romeo and Juliet

羅密歐與茱麗葉

商務印書館

This Chinese edition of *Romeo and Juliet*
has been published with the written permission of
Black Cat Publishing.

Name of Book: Romeo and Juliet CD-ROM
Author: William Shakespeare
Text adaptation, notes and activities: Derek Sellen
Dossier sections: Gina D. B. Clemen
Editors: Rebecca Raynes, Elvira Poggi Repetto
Design and art direction: Nadia Maestri
Computer graphics: Simona Corniola
Illustrations: Giovanni Manna
Picture Research: Laura Lagomarsino
Picture rights: © Manchester Art Gallery: 5; © The British Library: 6; By kind permission of the Marquess of Tavistock and Trustees of the Bedford Estate: 8; Derby Museums and Art Gallery: 9; Reproduction by courtesy of the National Gallery of Ireland: 68; Museo Nazionale di Capodimonte: 69; bfi Stills: 95
Edition: © 2003 Black Cat Publishing
an imprint of Cideb Editrice, Genoa, Canterbury

系 列 名：Black Cat 優質英語階梯閱讀 · Level 4
書　　名：羅密歐與茱麗葉 CD-ROM 版
責任編輯：黃淑嫻
封面設計：張毅　曹磊
出　　版：商務印書館（香港）有限公司
香港筲箕灣耀興道 3 號東滙廣場 8 樓
http://www.commercialpress.com.hk
印　　刷：中華商務彩色印刷有限公司
香港新界大埔汀麗路 36 號中華商務印刷大廈
版　　次：2015 年 4 月第 1 版第 3 次印刷
©2011 商務印書館（香港）有限公司
ISBN 978 962 07 1951 6
Printed in Hong Kong

出版說明

本館一向倡導優質閱讀，近年來連續推出了以“Q”為標識的“Quality English Learning 優質英語學習”系列，其中《讀名著學英語》叢書，更是香港書展入選好書，讀者反響令人鼓舞。推動社會閱讀風氣，推動英語經典閱讀，藉閱讀拓廣世界視野，提高英語水平，已經成為一種潮流。

然良好閱讀習慣的養成非一日之功，大多數初中級程度的讀者，常視直接閱讀厚重的原著為畏途。如何給年輕的讀者提供切實的指引和幫助，如何既提供優質的學習素材，又提供名師的教學方法，是當下社會關注的重要問題。針對這種情況，本館特別延請香港名校名師，根據多年豐富的教學經驗，精選海外適合初中級英語程度讀者的優質經典讀物，有系統地出版了這套叢書，名為《Black Cat 優質英語階梯閱讀》。

《Black Cat 優質英語階梯閱讀》體現了香港名校名師堅持經典學習的教學理念，以及多年行之有效的學習方法。既有經過改寫和縮寫的經典名著，又有富創意的現代作品；既有精心設計的聽、説、讀、寫綜合練習，又有豐富的歷史文化知識；既有彩色插圖、繪圖和照片，又有英美專業演員朗讀作品、含多種教學遊戲的 CD-ROM。適合口味不同的讀者享受閱讀之樂，欣賞經典之美。

《Black Cat 優質英語階梯閱讀》由淺入深，逐階提升，好像參與一個尋寶遊戲，入門並不難，但要真正尋得寶藏，需要投入，更需要堅持。只有置身其中的人，才能體味純正英語的魅力，領略得到真寶的快樂。當英語閱讀成為自己生活的一部分，英語水平的提高自然水到渠成。

商務印書館（香港）有限公司
編輯部

使用說明

1 應該怎樣選書？

按閱讀興趣選書

《Black Cat 優質英語階梯閱讀》精選世界經典作品，也包括富於創意的現代作品；既有膾炙人口的小說、戲劇，又有非小說類的文化知識讀物，品種豐富，內容多樣，適合口味不同的讀者挑選自己感興趣的書，享受閱讀的樂趣。

按英語程度選書

《Black Cat 優質英語階梯閱讀》現設Level 1 至 Level 6，由淺入深，涵蓋初、中級英語程度。讀物分級採用了國際上通用的劃分標準，主要以詞彙（vocabulary）和結構（structures）劃分。

Level 1 至 Level 3 出現的詞彙較淺顯，相對深的核心詞彙均配上中文解釋，節省讀者查找詞典的時間，以專心理解正文內容。在註釋的幫助下，讀者若能流暢地閱讀正文內容，就不用擔心這本書程度過深。

Level 1 至 Level 3出現的動詞時態形式和句子結構比較簡單。動詞時態形式以簡單現在式（present simple）、現在進行式（present continuous）、簡單過去式（past simple）為主，句子結構大部分是簡單句（simple sentences）。此外，還包括比較級和最高級（comparative and superlative forms）、可數和不可數名詞（countable and uncountable nouns）以及冠詞（articles）等語法知識點。

Level 4至 Level 6 出現的動詞時態形式，以現在完成式（present perfect）、現在完成進行式（present perfect continuous）、過去完成進行式（past perfect continuous）為主，句子結構大部分是複合句（compound sentences）、條件從句（1st and 2nd conditional sentences）等。此外，還包括情態動詞（modal verbs）、被動式（passive forms）、動名詞

（gerunds）、短語動詞（phrasal verbs）等語法知識點。

根據上述的語法範圍，讀者可按自己實際的英語水平，如詞彙量、語法知識、理解能力、閱讀能力等自主選擇，不再受制於學校年級劃分或學歷高低的約束，完全根據個人需要選擇合適的讀物。

2 怎樣提高閱讀效果？

閱讀的方法主要有兩種：一是泛讀，二是精讀。兩者各有功能，適當地結合使用，相輔相成，有事半功倍之效。

泛讀，指閱讀大量適合自己程度（可稍淺，但不能過深）、不同內容、風格、體裁的讀物，但求明白內容大意，不用花費太多時間鑽研細節，主要作用是多接觸英語，減輕對它的生疏感，鞏固以前所學過的英語，讓腦子在潛意識中吸收詞彙用法、語法結構等。

精讀，指小心認真地閱讀內容精彩、組織有條理、遣詞造句又正確的作品，着重點在於理解“準確”及“深入”，欣賞其精彩獨到之處。精讀時，可充分利用書中精心設計的練習，學習掌握有用的英語詞彙和語法知識。精讀後，可再花十分鐘朗讀其中一小段有趣的文字，邊唸邊細心領會文字的結構和意思。

《Black Cat 優質英語階梯閱讀》中的作品均值得精讀，如時間有限，不妨嘗試每兩個星期泛讀一本，輔以每星期挑選書中一章精彩的文字精讀。要學好英語，持之以恒地泛讀和精讀英文是最有效的方法。

3 本系列的練習與測試有何功能？

《Black Cat 優質英語階梯閱讀》特別注重練習的設計，為讀者考慮周到，切合實用需求，學習功能強。每章後均配有訓練聽、說、讀、寫四項技能的練習，分量、難度恰到好處。

聽力練習分兩類，一是重聽故事回答問題，二是聆聽主角對話、書信朗讀、或模擬記者訪問後寫出答案，旨在以生活化的練習形式逐步提高聽力。每本書均配有 CD-ROM 提供作品朗讀，朗讀者都是專業演員，英國作品由英國演員錄音，美國作品由美國演員錄音，務求增加聆聽的真實感和感染力。多聆聽英式和美式英語兩種發音，可讓讀者熟悉二者的差異，逐漸培養分辨英美發音的能力，提高聆聽理解的準確度。此外，模仿錄音朗讀故事或模仿主人翁在戲劇中的對白，都是訓練口語能力的好方法。

除了作品朗讀，CD-ROM 亦附有多種教學遊戲，讓讀者學習生字、造句和讀音等。遊戲練習形式多樣化，有縱橫字謎、配對、填空、字句重組等等，注重訓練讀者的理解、推敲和聯想等多種閱讀技能。透過圖像、聲音、短片的多媒體教學，可增加做練習的趣味，加強讀者對本書內容的印象，更有效地學習。

書內的寫作練習尤具新意，教讀者使用網式圖示（spidergrams）記錄重點，採用問答、書信、電報、記者採訪等多樣化形式，鼓勵讀者動手寫作。

書後更設有升級測試（Exit Test）及答案，供讀者檢查學習效果。充分利用書中的練習和測試，可全面提升聽、説、讀、寫四項技能。

4 本系列還能提供甚麼幫助？

《Black Cat 優質英語階梯閱讀》提倡豐富多元的現代閱讀，巧用書中提供的資訊，有助於提升英語理解力，擴闊視野。

每本書都設有專章介紹相關的歷史文化知識，經典名著更附有作者生平、社會背景等資訊。書內富有表現力的彩色插圖、繪圖和照片，使閱讀充滿趣味，部分加上如何解讀古典名畫的指導，增長見識。有的書還提供一些與主題相關的網址，比如關於不同國家的節慶源流的網址，讓讀者多利用網上資源增進知識。

CONTENTS

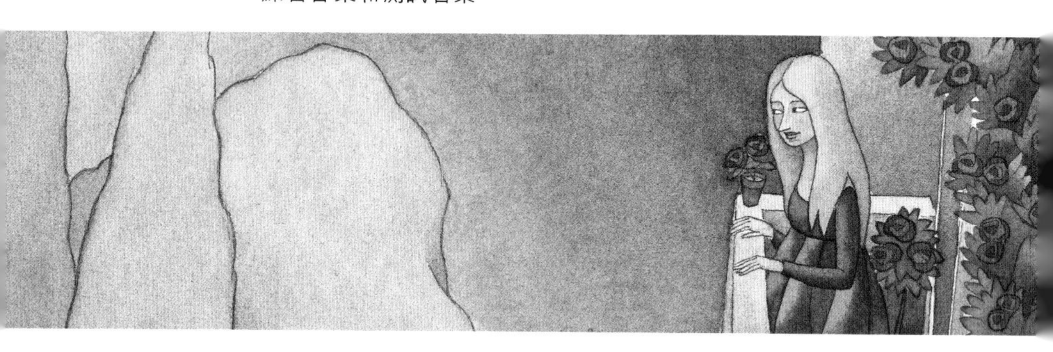

PET Cambridge **P**reliminary **E**nglish **T**est-style exercises

T: GRADES 5, 6 Trinity-style exercises (Grades 5, 6)

This story is recorded in full. 故事錄音

 This symbol indicates the chapters and exercises featured on the accompanying CD. 文章和聽力練習的錄音標記

William Shakespeare (1800-1803) by William Blake.

Shakespeare's Life

William Shakespeare was born in Stratford-upon-Avon in the English Midlands on St George's Day, April 23rd, 1564. (St George is the patron saint of England.) He was the third child of John Shakespeare, a glove-maker, who was an important man in the town, and Mary Arden. He went to Stratford Grammar School, where he received a good education, but he had no university education.

In 1582, when he was only eighteen, he married Anne Hathaway. They had three children – Hamnet, a boy who died when he was only eleven years old, Susanna and Judith. As far as we know, they were happily married. When he died he left his 'second-best bed' to his wife in his will. [1] Perhaps it was their marriage bed.

Very little is known about Shakespeare's later life. There is a legend that he had to leave Stratford because he was caught stealing a deer. [2]

Shakespeare went to London and became involved [3] in the world of the theatre. Drama then was as important a part of life as television is for us. All classes of society enjoyed the plays by Shakespeare and other Elizabethan dramatists.

1. **will** : a document written before someone dies.
2. **deer** : 
3. **involved** : interested.

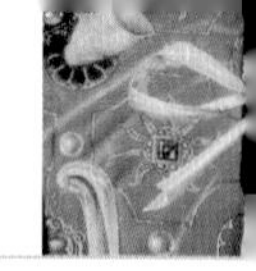

Detail of *The View of London* (1650), by Claes Jansz Visscher.

Did you know that in Shakespeare's theatre, boys played the parts of women? Juliet, Cleopatra, Desdemona and Lady Macbeth were all played by young men whose voices had not broken. Actresses were not allowed on the English stage until late in the following century.

Shakespeare quickly became very popular as a writer. One of his rivals [1] called him a 'crow' [2] who had stolen the 'feathers' [3] of the other writers.

His friend, Ben Jonson, wrote that he was 'honest, open and free'. Another writer said that he was 'handsome', 'well-shaped' and had a 'pleasant smooth wit'. [4]

Apart from the plays, he also wrote a collection of sonnets. Many of these poems are written to a 'Dark Lady', but nobody can discover her identity.

1. **rivals** : competitors.
2. **crow** : an ugly black bird. 
3. **feathers** :
4. **wit** : ability to use words to produce a clever type of humour.

We do not know very much about Shakespeare's personal life but plays such as *Romeo and Juliet* show that he was very interested in the theme of passionate [1] love.

When Shakespeare died – on his birthday in 1616 – he was buried in Stratford. There are four lines written on his tombstone, including these:

Blessed [2] is the man who spares [3] these stones.
And cursed [4] is the man who moves my bones.

Perhaps these lines show that Shakespeare did not want us to know about his personal life. Instead, he has left us his poems and plays.

An inside view of the Globe Theatre where Shakespeare acted.

1. **passionate** : having very strong feelings.
2. **blessed** : happy, lucky.
3. **spares** : does not touch.
4. **cursed** : unlucky, unhappy.

Shakespeare and Romeo and Juliet

Shakespeare wrote *Romeo and Juliet* in the middle of the 1590s. Elizabeth the First was Queen of England. During her reign, [1] the country had made great progress in many different areas – travelling by sea, exploration, war, music, architecture, drama and poetry. England had become a major power in Europe and had defeated the Spanish Armada in 1588 when Philip the Second had attempted to invade the country.

In all the arts, there was great influence from Italy. The Renaissance had begun in Italy and the English were very enthusiastic [2] about Italian culture. Chaucer, the first important English poet, respected Dante as the greatest European poet. The most popular form of love poetry, the sonnet, was 'borrowed' [3] from Italian writers. Many of Shakespeare's plays are located in

The Armada Portrait of Queen Elizabeth I (*c.* 1588) by George Gower, Woburn Abbey.

1. **reign** : the period when a king or queen has power.
2. **enthusiastic** : showing strong interest.
3. **borrowed** : taken.

Italy and based on Italian stories. For the English, Italy was the country of passion, vendettas, [1] murder, suicide and deep emotion. When Shakespeare wanted to write a tragedy of love and death, he chose an Italian story.
The legend of Romeo and Juliet had been very popular in England for a long time. Shakespeare took the story, changed some of the details and made it into a great play with characters which live in the memory. He changed the age of Juliet; in his play, she is only thirteen years old. It was possible to get married at twelve or thirteen but most people in Elizabethan society waited until later. 'Arranged marriages' were normal. In other words, the family decided who their sons and daughters should marry. There are many stories about the conflict [2] between the wishes of the parents and the romantic feelings of their children.

Romeo and Juliet (1790-1791) by Joseph Wright Derby.

1. **vendettas** : long-lasting quarrels between families.
2. **conflict** : argument.

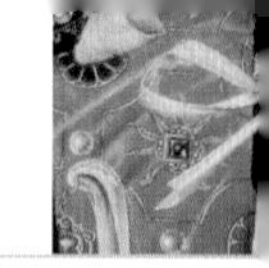

Romeo and Juliet has the reputation of being the perfect love story. But it is not only about love. It is also about the hate between the Montagues and the Capulets. It ends, not in marriage, but in death. The lovers are very young. Romeo changes his mind easily; at the beginning of the play, he loves Rosaline, not Juliet. He often acts without thinking and he kills two people. Juliet also changes her mind. She thinks she is too young to get married but when she sees Romeo...!!!

The story of Romeo and Juliet has lived until the present day. Other writers and musical composers have produced their own interpretations [1] of the old, old story. But Shakespeare was the first one to make a great work of dramatic art from the story of the 'star-crossed [2] lovers' who lived in Renaissance Verona.

A scene from the Royal Ballet's version of *Romeo and Juliet*.

SUMMARY

In the beautiful city of Verona, there are two families who hate each other. When Romeo from the Montagues and Juliet from the Capulets fall in love, it creates problems for everybody. Friar Laurence, kind and optimistic, [3] *tries to help the young lovers. But there are other people in Verona, such as Tybalt, the 'Prince of Cats', who want to destroy the peace of the city. 'True Love' has to fight to survive...*

1. **interpretations** : explanations or opinions.
2. **star-crossed** : unlucky.
3. **optimistic** : believing that good things will happen.

1 **How much do you remember about Shakespeare? Complete the summary by choosing the correct words.**

William Shakespeare was born in 1 **1564/1664/1774**. He was the 2 **fourth/first/third** child of John Shakespeare, a 3 **glove-maker/painter/doctor**. When he was eighteen he married Anne Hathaway and they had 4 **three/four/two** children.

5 **A lot/Some/Only a little** is known about Shakespeare's life. There is a legend that he had to leave Stratford because he was caught stealing a 6 **deer/cow/dog**. He went to 7 **Leeds/Liverpool/London** and became involved in the theatre.

He became very popular as a(n) 8 **actor/writer/singer** and one of his rivals accused him of 9 **copying/helping/criticizing** other writers.

As well as his plays he wrote a collection of 10 **poems/novels/reviews**. Many of these were written to a 'Dark Lady'.

Shakespeare died on 11 **Christmas Day/his wedding anniversary/his birthday** in 1616 and he was buried in 12 **London/Stratford/Stirling**.

PET **2** **Look at the statements below about Shakespeare and *Romeo and Juliet*. Read pages 12-14 and decide if each statement is correct or incorrect. If it is correct, mark A. If it is incorrect, mark B.**

		A	B
1.	*Romeo and Juliet* was written in the middle of the 1950s.	☐	☐
2.	In the arts, there was great influence from Italy.	☐	☐
3.	Dante respected Chaucer as the greatest European poet.	☐	☐
4.	All of Shakespeare's plays are located in Italy.	☐	☐
5.	In England the people had never heard of the legend of Romeo and Juliet.	☐	☐
6.	Shakespeare changed some of the details for his version.	☐	☐
7.	In his play Juliet is only seventeen years old.	☐	☐
8.	Arranged marriages were normal in Elizabethan society.	☐	☐
9.	*Romeo and Juliet* is about love and hate.	☐	☐
10.	The story ends happily.	☐	☐

3 **Correct the statements you have marked as false (B) in 2.**

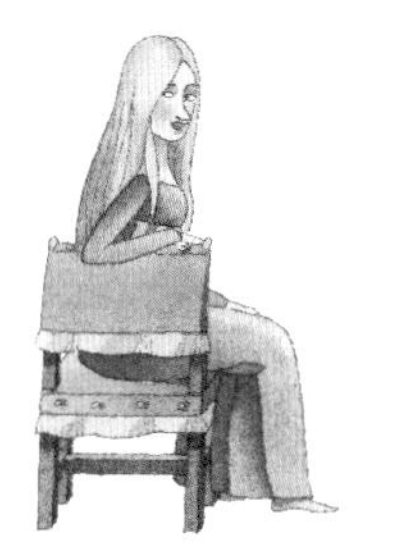

Dramatis Personae

Romeo	the only son of the Montague family
Juliet	the only daughter of the Capulet family
The Prince	the governor of Verona
Lord Capulet	Juliet's father
Lady Capulet	Juliet's mother
Lord Montague	Romeo's father
Lady Montague	Romeo's mother
Benvolio	Romeo's cousin
Tybalt	Juliet's cousin
Mercutio	Romeo's friend
Paris	a friend of the Prince and of the Capulets
The Nurse	
Friar Laurence	
Friar John	
Balthasar	Romeo's servant
Servants	

PART ONE

THE MONTAGUES AND THE CAPULETS

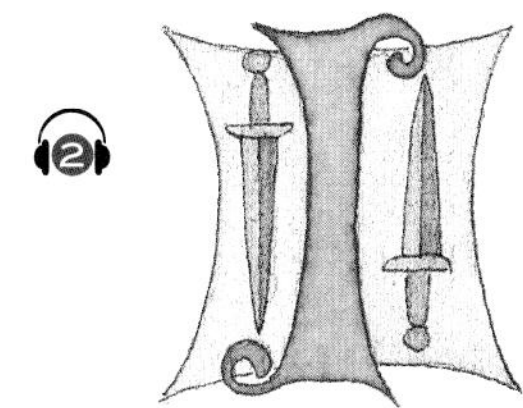

In the beautiful city of Verona, there were two families – the Montagues and the Capulets. They hated [1] each other. They had hated each other for hundreds of years.

One day, two servants of the house of Capulet were walking in the streets.

'If I meet any man or woman from the house of Montague, I'll push them out of the way,' said Sampson.

1. **hated** : didn't like.

'No, you'll run away,' laughed his friend, Gregory.

'Don't worry about that,' said Sampson. 'I will stand and fight.'

Just then, two servants from the house of Montague came into the same street.

Sampson took out his sword [1] and bit his thumb [2] at them. This was a great insult. [3] The two groups of servants began to fight.

'The Montagues are better than the Capulets,' shouted the servants of the Montagues.

'Our masters, the Capulets, are better,' shouted the servants of the Capulets.

Then Benvolio, a member of the Montague family, arrived. He tried to make peace.

'Stop, fools! [4] Put away your swords.'

But no-one listened to him. The servants continued fighting and Benvolio took out his sword to stop them. Then Tybalt arrived. He was a Capulet, the most dangerous member of the family. He loved fighting.

'Benvolio, you have drawn your sword. [5] Now you must fight with me. Look at your death!'

'I am only trying to separate these fools,' replied Benvolio. 'Put away your sword or use it to help me keep the peace.'

'Peace!' snarled [6] Tybalt. 'I hate the word. I hate all Montagues and I hate you!'

With those words, Tybalt attacked Benvolio with his sword.

1. **sword**:
2. **thumb** : the largest finger, 'biting your thumb' was a great insult in this period of history.
3. **insult** : a rude action.
4. **fools** : stupid people.
5. **drawn your sword** : taken out your sword.
6. **snarled** : said in a fierce angry way.

Then Lord and Lady Capulet arrived. Lord Capulet was old but he wanted to fight too. 'Bring me my sword,' he shouted.

'You are too old to fight,' said Lady Capulet. 'You don't need a sword, you need a crutch.' [1]

Then Lord and Lady Montague arrived. Lord Montague was swinging [2] his sword although his wife tried to stop him.

More and more people came. Soon everyone was fighting. It was very dangerous.

At last, the Prince of Verona arrived. He was very angry.

'Stop fighting! I want peace in my city! Drop your weapons [3] or you will all die! This is the third time that your families have been fighting in the streets.

'Lord Capulet and Lord Montague, you are old but you are not wise. You must promise not to fight. Lord Capulet, come with me now. We must talk. Lord Montague, come to see me this afternoon. If your two families fight again, you will both die!'

Everyone went away except the Montagues. The fight was over.

'How did it begin?' Lord Montague asked Benvolio.

'The servants were fighting. I drew my sword to stop them. Then Tybalt arrived. He began fighting with me. Soon everyone was involved.' [4]

'Where is my son, Romeo? Is he safe?' asked Lady Montague.

'I saw him this morning, an hour before the sunrise,' replied Benvolio. 'He was walking alone in the fields. He saw me but he didn't want my company. [5] He went into the forest.'

Lord Montague nodded. [6] 'People have often seen him there in the morning. He cries. Then he comes home and locks himself in his

1. **a crutch** : something to help an old person to walk.

2. **swinging** : moving violently.
3. **weapons** : objects used in fighting.
4. **involved** : part of the fight.
5. **company** : being together with somebody.
6. **nodded** : moved the head down and up again quickly.

room. He shuts out the daylight and spends all his time alone in the dark. Something is wrong.'

'Have you questioned him?'

'Yes, but he gives no answer.'

'But look, he is coming now,' said Benvolio. 'I will ask him about his problems.'

'I hope he will answer you. We will leave you to speak privately,' [1] said Lord Montague.

Romeo was on his way back from the forest to the city.

'Good morning, cousin,' said Benvolio.

'It is a sad morning,' replied Romeo.

'Why? Why are your days sad and long?'

'I am...'

'In love?'

'Out...'

'Out of love?'

'Out of my lady's favour. I love her but she does not love me. Love is a terrible thing, Benvolio. I love and I hate. Love comes from nothing. It is heavy and light, serious and foolish, hot and cold, sick and healthy. Are you laughing at me?'

'No, I am sad because you are sad.'

'Love is a madness. [2] Goodbye, cousin.'

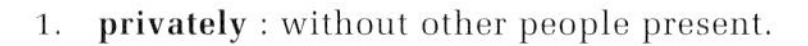

1. **privately** : without other people present.
2. **madness** : craziness.

'Tell me, who do you love?'

'I love a woman.'

'I know that. But who?'

'I love sweet Rosaline. She is beautiful, intelligent [1] and good. But she does not love me.'

'Forget her. There are many other girls.'

'No, I can never forget her.'

Lord Capulet decided to have a party.

'I will invite all the important people from Verona. But not the Montagues.'

He wanted his daughter, Juliet, to meet Paris, a lord from Verona, the friend of the Prince. He hoped she would marry Paris in the future. He called for his servant.

'Here is a list of names. Go and invite the guests.' [2]

The servant met Romeo and Benvolio in the street. He did not know that they were Montagues. 'Can you

1. **intelligent** : clever.
2. **guests** : the people invited to a party.

help me?' he asked. 'I can't read the names on this piece of paper.'

'Look, Romeo. Rosaline will be at the party.'

'I have an idea,' said Romeo suddenly. [1]

Meanwhile, [2] Lady Capulet was talking to Juliet, her thirteen-year-old daughter. Juliet had an old nurse who looked after her. [3]

'You will meet Paris at the party,' Lady Capulet told Juliet. 'Perhaps you will marry him one day.'

'Mother, I am too young to get married,' replied Juliet.

'I would love to see my little Juliet married,' said the Nurse. 'You will have happy days and happy nights.'

1. **suddenly** : very quickly, with no warning.
2. **Meanwhile** : at the same time.
3. **looked after her** : cared for her, helped her.

Comprehension and Opinion

1 What happened in Part One?

a. What are the names of the two families?
b. Did Benvolio and Tybalt want the same thing?
c. Why was the Prince angry?
d. Why was Romeo unhappy?
e. How did Romeo and Benvolio get information about the party?
f. Why did Lord and Lady Capulet want Juliet to meet Paris?

What do you think?

What will happen next? What is Romeo's idea?

Using Adjectives

2 a. Can you remember the adjectives which are used in the story? Fill in these gaps.

a. In the _ _ _ _ _ _ _ _ _ city of Verona, there were two families.
b. Tybalt was the most _ _ _ _ _ _ _ _ _ member of the Capulet family.
c. Lord Capulet was _ _ _ but he wanted to fight too.
d. The Prince was very _ _ _ _ _ .
e. 'You are _ _ _ but you are not _ _ _ _ .'
f. 'Why are your days _ _ _ and _ _ _ _ ?'
g. Love is a _ _ _ _ _ _ _ _ thing.
h. Love is also _ _ _ _ _ and _ _ _ _ _, _ _ _ _ _ _ _ and _ _ _ _ _ _ _ .
i. 'Rosaline is _ _ _ _ _ _ _ _ _ , _ _ _ _ _ _ _ _ _ _ _ and _ _ _ _ .'
j. 'You will have _ _ _ _ _ days and _ _ _ _ _ nights.'

b. Make a chain [1] of adjectives. Use the last letter to begin the next adjective.

For example:
dangerou**s**-**s**tupi**d**-**d**ifficul**t**-**t**al**l**-**l**ou**d**-**d**angerous

How many words can you include in your chain?

c. Opposites（相反詞）

Romeo uses adjectives with opposite meanings to describe love: 'Love is heavy and light, serious and foolish, hot and cold, sick and healthy.' Look at these adjectives:

~~beautiful~~	cruel	fat	friendly	hard-working	
happy	intelligent	kind	lazy	modest	poor
proud	rich	sad	short	stupid	tall
terrible	thin	~~ugly~~	unfriendly	wonderful	

Beautiful and *ugly* are opposites.

There are ten more pairs of opposites in the box. What are they?

0. beautiful / ugly
1. ....
2. ....
3. ....
4. ....
5. ....
6. ....
7. ....
8. ....
9. ....
10. ....

Now use some of these adjectives to describe people you know.

....
....
....

1. chain : 

d. **Synonyms**（同義詞）

Sometimes there are adjectives which have the same or similar meanings. These are called *synonyms*. Here are six words:

happy	
sad	
rich	
beautiful	
wonderful	
thin	

Which words in the box below have similar meanings? There are three synonyms for each word above. Fill in the table.

affluent attractive depressed ecstatic
slim excellent fantastic great glad handsome
joyful miserable pretty prosperous skinny
slender unhappy wealthy

N.B. There are often special uses for adjectives:

For example:
Prosperous and **affluent** are formal words.
Skinny is negative but **slim** is positive.
Handsome is usually used for men or boys.
Ecstatic is stronger than **happy**.

'Too' with an Adjective

3 **In the story, Juliet says: 'I am too young to get married.' Lady Capulet says: 'You are too old to fight.'**
How many more sentences can you make? Use: ' ***... too... to...*** **'**
Use the words below.

a. lazy	to carry
b. tired	to drive a car
c. fat	to go shopping
d. young	to dance
e. cold	to study
f. ill	to go to bed
g. unhappy	to wear this dress
h. late	to pass the test
i. early	to go to the beach
j. heavy	to eat dinner
k. stupid	to learn English
l. poor	to make a mistake
m. intelligent	to play football

For example:

It's too late to go shopping.
She's too tired to study.
He's too lazy to carry this suitcase.

Now practise questions and answers with a friend:

Why don't you go shopping? It's too late.
Why don't you study? I'm too tired.

Families

4 Complete these words. Each word is the name of a member of a family.

a. Romeo is Lord Montague's
b. My father's sister is my
c. Juliet is Lady Capulet's
d. Lord Montague is Romeo's
e. Benvolio is Romeo's
f. Lady Capulet is Juliet's
g. Romeo is an only child. He has no
h. He has no
i. Romeo has two
j. Lady Capulet is Lord Capulet's
k. He is her
l. My father's brother is my
m. My mother's mother is my
n. My sister's son is my

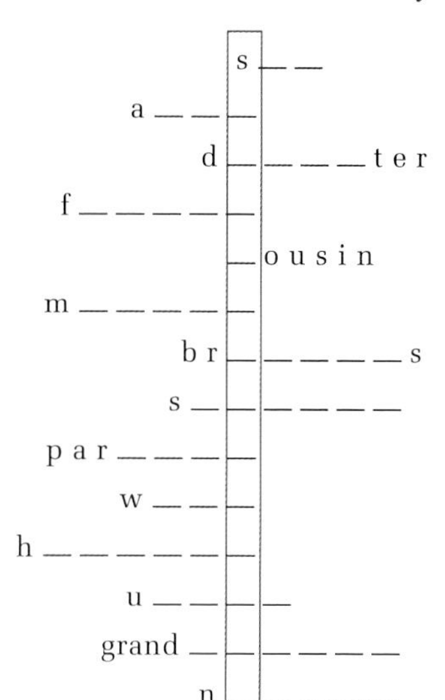

Now read DOWN from the letter 's' in the first line.
Put the letters in these spaces:

S _ _ _ - _ _ _ _ _ _ _ _ _ _ _ V _ R S

This is Shakespeare's description of Romeo and Juliet. The first word means 'unlucky'.

The Queen of the Fairies[1]

PET **5** **Look at the six sentences below. You will hear a conversation between Romeo and his friend Mercutio. Decide if each sentence is correct or incorrect. If it is correct, put a tick (✓) in the box under A for YES. If it is not correct, put a tick (✓) in the box under B for NO.**

	A	B
1. Mercutio thinks that Romeo is deeply in love.	☐	☐
2. Romeo dreamt about Juliet last night.	☐	☐
3. Queen Mab is a real person.	☐	☐
4. Mercutio says that Queen Mab keeps us awake.	☐	☐
5. Mercutio says that Queen Mab visits girls, soldiers and lovers.	☐	☐
6. Mercutio thinks that Queen Mab is very powerful.	☐	☐

6 **Now rewrite the incorrect sentences.**

....

....

....

7 **In exercise 5 Romeo and Mercutio talk about dreams. Think of any books you have read / films you have seen which have dreams in them:**

- did the dreams come true?
- were the dreams frightening?
- how was the dream told / shown?

Discuss with your friend(s).

a. Do you often have dreams?
b. Do you dream in colour or black and white?
c. Do you have nightmares?[2]
d. Do you have re-occurring dreams?
e. Do you think that dreams can come true?
f. Think of the last vivid[3] dream you had and describe it to your friend(s).

1. **fairies** : a fairy is a small magical creature with wings.
2. **nightmares** : frightening dreams.
3. **vivid** : producing clear pictures in the mind.

The Verona Times

PET **8** **This is part of a letter that a citizen of Verona receives from a friend:**

... In your next letter, please tell me all the news from Verona.
I heard that there was a street fight. Is it true? Why did it happen?

Now the citizen is writing a letter to this friend. Write the citizen's letter in about 100 words.
Explain about the Montagues and the Capulets. Describe the fight and give the Prince's decision.

9 **Your friend has asked you to predict what will happen at the Capulets' party. Write the story of the party; then read or listen to Part Two to see if you were close to what really happened.**
Your story must begin with this sentence:

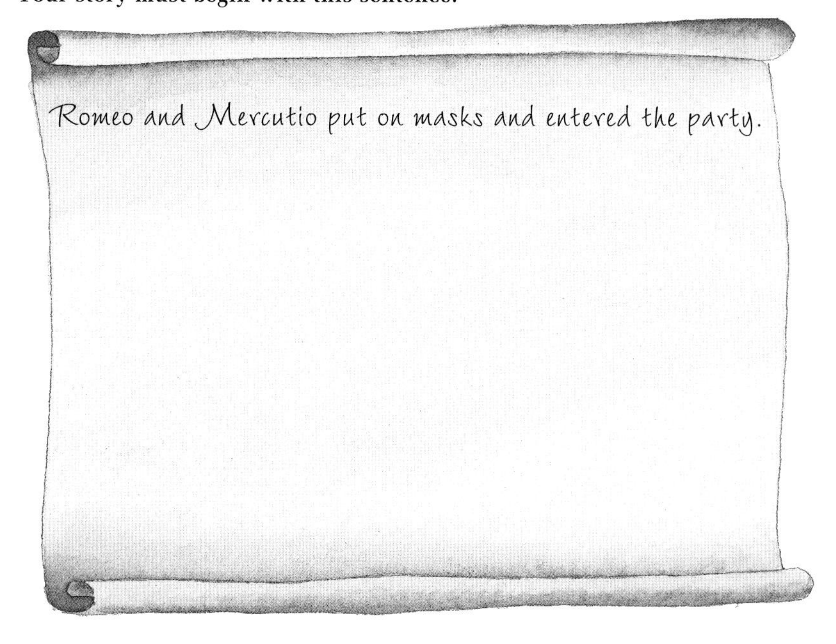

Write your story in about 100 words.

PART TWO

THE GARDEN OF THE CAPULETS

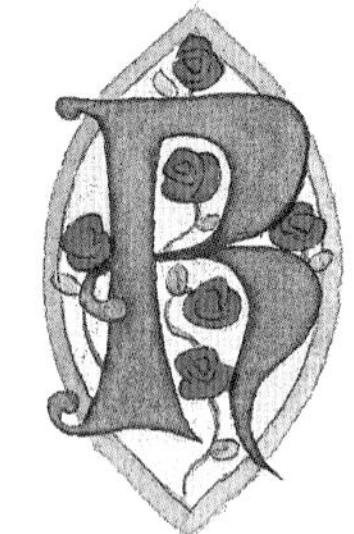

Romeo went to the party with Benvolio and his friend, Mercutio. They were all wearing masks. [1] It was very dangerous for the Montagues and their friends to go to a party in the house of the Capulets.

'I cannot wait [2] to see fair [3] Rosaline,' said Romeo as they approached [4] the house.

Lord Capulet welcomed them. 'Come in, gentlemen. Dance and drink and eat. Enjoy yourselves.' He did not recognise the son of his enemy, Lord Montague.

1. **masks** : coverings for faces.
2. **I cannot wait** : I am very excited.
3. **fair** : beautiful.
4. **approached** : came near.

He spoke to all the guests. 'Now, girls, dance to the music. When I was younger, I whispered [1] sweet things in the ears of the ladies. But now I am old. My dancing days are finished. I will sit here with the old people and talk about the past.'

As they went into the house, Romeo saw Juliet for the first time. He forgot Rosaline! He fell in love!

'Who is that lady?' asked Romeo. 'She is more beautiful than the moon. She is like a bright jewel [2] in the darkness. She is like a dove [3] among crows. I have never loved until now.'

But Tybalt recognised Romeo's voice. 'It is a Montague. Bring me my sword. It is a great insult for a Montague to come here to laugh at our party. I will kill him.'

'What's the matter, Tybalt?' asked Lord Capulet.

'That man in the mask is a Montague, uncle.'

'Be calm, Tybalt. Is it Romeo? He has a good reputation in Verona. This is a party. I want no trouble [4] in my house. Let him enjoy himself.'

'No, uncle. He is our enemy.'

'Don't be cheeky, [5] young man. I am the master in this house. You must do as I say.'

Tybalt did not agree but he did not want to make Lord Capulet angry. 'I will leave the party. I cannot stay here with a Montague in the room. But I will not forget. Romeo will have a good time tonight but tomorrow he will pay!'

Romeo went to Juliet and talked to her. He did not know who she was. He took her hand gently in his.

'My lips are ready to kiss you,' he said softly.

1. **whispered** : spoke softly.
2. **jewel** : for example, a diamond or a pearl.
3. **dove** : a beautiful white bird.
4. **trouble** : problems.
5. **cheeky** : rude.

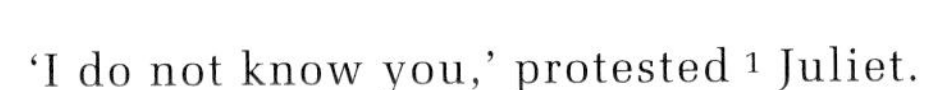

'I do not know you,' protested [1] Juliet.

'I must kiss you,' insisted [2] Romeo.

'Here I am,' said Juliet. 'My lips are here.'

Romeo kissed Juliet. He kissed her a second time.

Then the Nurse came to take Juliet to her mother.

'That is Juliet. She is a Capulet,' the Nurse told Romeo.

Romeo was very surprised and upset. [3] He was in love with the daughter of the enemy of his family.

'Quickly, let's go,' said Benvolio. 'It is dangerous here.'

Juliet asked the Nurse, 'Who is that young man?'

'That is Romeo. He is a Montague.'

Juliet was also very surprised and upset. She was in love with the son of the enemy of her family. 'We can never get married,' she thought.

After they left the party, Mercutio and Benvolio looked for Romeo.

'Look! He is there in the shadows. [4] What is he doing?' said Mercutio.

'He is jumping [5] the wall. He is going into the garden of the Capulets.'

Mercutio called out. 'Romeo! Madman! Lover! He is going to look for Rosaline.'

'Quiet! You will make him angry,' said Benvolio. 'His love is blind.' [6]

Mercutio laughed. 'Good night, Romeo. He is probably sitting under a tree, dreaming about that girl. He is mad.'

Mercutio and Benvolio went home. The night was silent.

In the dark garden, Romeo suddenly saw a light. Juliet was standing on her balcony. 'She is beautiful,' he thought. 'Her eyes are stars. They give light to the night. Her glove touches her cheek [7] – I would like to be her glove!'

1. **protested** : complained.
2. **insisted** : demanded forcefully.
3. **upset** : sad, confused.
4. **shadows** : dark places without light.
5. **jumping** : going over.
6. **blind** : unable to see.
7. **cheek** : the side of the face.

Juliet began to speak to the night. She did not know that Romeo was listening.

'Ah, Romeo,' she sighed. [1]

'Speak again, angel,' he whispered.

'O Romeo, Romeo! Why is your name Romeo?
Let's change our names. Then we can love.
Forget that you are a Montague.
Or, if you love me, I will not be a Capulet.
Montague and Capulet are only names.
A rose can have any name. It always smells sweet.'

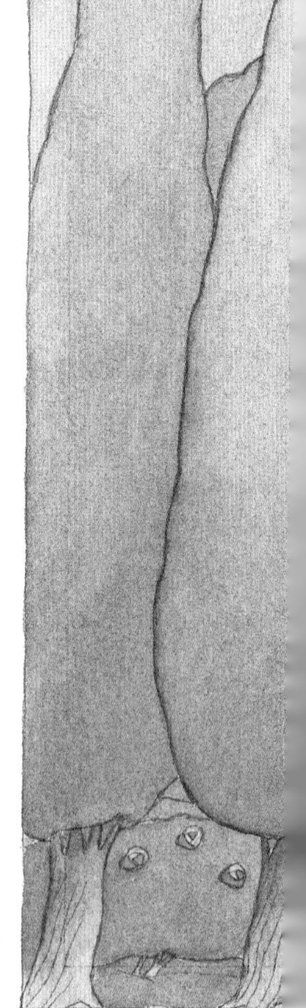

Romeo called out. [2] 'I will change my name for you.'

'Who's there?' asked Juliet. 'Who is listening in the middle of the night?'

'I will not tell you my name because it is your enemy.'

'I know your voice. Are you Romeo? But how did you get over the garden wall?'

'Love gave me wings. [3] No walls can shut out love.'

'If my family find you, they will murder you.'

'The night hides me. I am safe. Love has sent me here to you.'

Romeo and Juliet talked together. Romeo knew Juliet's secret – she loved him. They decided to get married secretly.

'Will you be true?' [4] asked Juliet.

'Yes, my darling,' replied Romeo. 'I promise by the moon.'

'But the moon changes. Will your love change?'

'Never. I will always love you. Do you love me?'

'I told the night that I loved you and you heard me. But I wish I had been silent.'

'Have you changed your mind?' [5]

1. **sighed** : breathed heavily.
2. **called out** : spoke loudly.
3. **wings** :
4. **true** : faithful, loyal.
5. **changed your mind** : changed your idea.

'No, my love is as deep as the sea. But I must go. The Nurse is calling. Good night, Romeo.'

'Good night, Juliet.'

The Nurse called: 'Juliet! Juliet!'

'I'm coming, Nurse. Good night.'

'Good night.'

'It is very sad and very sweet to say good night. But tomorrow, we will be married.'

Comprehension and Opinion

1 What happened in Part Two?

a. Why were Romeo and his friends wearing masks?
b. What happened when Romeo saw Juliet?
c. What did Romeo and Juliet do?
d. How did Romeo enter the garden?
e. Where was Juliet?
f. What did Romeo and Juliet decide to do?

What do you think?

Will Romeo and Juliet get married?
Will they be happy? Do they really love each other?

Use of Adverbs

We use adverbs to describe actions. They usually end in '-ly'.

For example: *They will get married* ***secretly***.

Adjectives ending in **'-ic'** usually add **'-ally'**.
For example: *How did Mercutio talk about Romeo?* ***Sarcastically***.

A few adverbs do not end in **'-ly'**.
For example: *He ran* ***fast***. *They worked* ***hard***.

2 Complete the sentences below with suitable adverbs from the box:

angrily	anxiously	beautifully	comically
immediately	kindly	loudly	lovingly
passionately	sadly	stupidly	violently

a. Romeo fell in love with Juliet ....
b. The Prince spoke ....
c. Benvolio behaved ....

d. Tybalt fought ....

e. The Nurse called ....

f. Juliet thought about Romeo ....

g. The servants behaved ....

h. Romeo and Juliet loved each other ....

i. At the party, Juliet danced ....

j. Lady Montague asked about Romeo ....

Past Simple（過去時）and Past Continuous（過去進行時）

Look at this sentence:

While Romeo ***was looking*** *for Rosaline, he* ***saw*** *Juliet.*

The first action continued for a long time:
'Romeo was looking...' (Past Continuous)

The second action happened suddenly, during this time:
'he saw...' (Past Simple)

3 Now put the verbs in these sentences in the Past Continuous (*was/were -ing*) or Past Simple form. Remember that some verbs have an irregular past form (e.g. *see* → *saw*).

a. While Benvolio *(try)* to stop the fight, Tybalt *(arrive)*.

b. The Prince *(see)* that everybody *(fight)*.

c. Benvolio *(walk)* near the forest when he *(meet)* Romeo.

d. The Nurse *(help)* Juliet when her mother *(come)* into the room.

e. While Romeo and Juliet *(kiss)*, the Nurse *(see)* them.

f. Tybalt *(recognise)* Romeo's voice while he *(talk)*.

g. While Romeo *(stand)* in the garden, Juliet *(begin)* to speak.

h. While Juliet *(say)* goodbye to Romeo, the Nurse *(call)*.

Here are some examples from a modern love story:

i. Juliet *(use)* her computer when Romeo *(phone)* her.

j. While her parents *(watch)* TV, Juliet *(leave)* the house.

k. Romeo *(not want)* to meet Juliet because his favourite team *(play)* football.

l. Juliet *(not answer)* the phone because she *(watch)* a video.

m. While Tybalt and Benvolio *(fight)*, the police *(arrive)*.

Love and Marriage

4 In Shakespeare's play, Juliet says good night to Romeo with these words:

1 2 3 4 5 6 7   5 8   8 9 10 11
__ __ __ __ __ __ __   __ __   __ __ __ __

8 12 13 13 4   8 14 3 3 14 12
__ __ __ __ __   __ __ __ __ __ __

Each number represents a letter of the alphabet.
If you can find the words in the gaps below, you will be able to know what Juliet said.

For example: The answer for number **1** is 'RING'.
Therefore, 3 = R 5 = I 6 = N 7 = G

1. A married woman wears this on her finger: __ __ __ __ (3 5 6 7)
2. When people get married there is a: __ __ D D __ __ __ (12 13 _ _ 5 6 7)
3. The woman who gets married is the: B __ __ D __ (3 5 _ 13)
4. The man who gets married is the: B __ __ D __ __ __ __ __ M (3 5 _ 13 7 3 14 14)
5. They usually get married in a: __ __ __ __ __ __ (10 11 9 3 10 11)
6. They are married in church by a: __ __ __ __ __ __ (1 3 5 13 8 4)
7. Everybody hopes the couple will be: __ __ __ __ Y (11 2 1 1)
8. But sometimes marriages end in: D __ V __ __ __ __ (5 _ 14 3 10 13)
9. Romeo and Juliet will marry: __ __ __ __ __ __ L Y (8 13 10 3 13 4)
10. Sometimes people have a broken: __ __ __ __ __ (11 13 2 3 4)
11. Romeo and Juliet were in: L __ V __ (14 _ 13)
12. They fell in love at first: __ __ G __ __ (8 5 _ 11 4)
13. Rosaline was Romeo's first: G __ __ L F __ __ __ __ D (5 3 _ _ 3 5 13 6)

Do you understand Juliet's words?

T: GRADE 6

5 **TOPIC – CLOTHES AND CELEBRATIONS**
Bring a photograph or some pictures of a wedding in your country. Talk to your friend(s) and include information on the following:

a. What clothes did the bride and bridegroom wear?
b. What did other people wear?
c. What food and drink did you have?
d. What was the music and atmosphere like?

The Party

PET **6** **There are seven questions in this exercise. For each question there are three pictures. As you listen to the recording choose the correct picture and tick (✓) in the box below it.**

Example: Where is the speaker standing?

A ✓ B ☐ C ☐

1. Where is Lord Capulet standing?

A ☐ B ☐ C ☐

2. Who have just arrived at the party?

A ☐

B ☐

C ☐

3. Where is Juliet?

A ☐

B ☐

C ☐

4. What is the Nurse looking at?

A ☐

B ☐

C ☐

5. How many servants are there?

A ☐ 

B ☐ 

C ☐ 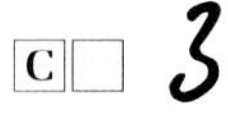

6. Who is on the balcony?

A ☐   B ☐   C ☐

7. Which of these is not at the party?

A ☐   B ☐   C ☐

8. What is the reporter's question?

9. What is the correct answer? You can check your answer on page 116.

7 **Romeo saw Juliet at the party and spoke to her in the garden. Write the note which Romeo sends to Juliet next day. In the note, you should**

- tell Juliet how much you love her
- tell her why you love her – because she's beautiful etc.
- arrange to meet her again

Write 35 – 45 words.

8 **An English friend of yours called Tom likes Shakespeare very much. You want to invite him to a performance of *Romeo and Juliet*.**
Write a card to Tom. In the card, you should

- invite him to come to the theatre
- tell him the date and time of the performance
- ask him to let you know if he wants to come

Write 35 – 45 words.

PET **9** **At the time of *Romeo and Juliet*, women did not have the opportunity of a career, so several of Juliet's friends are looking for men to marry.**
On page 45 there are some descriptions of single men.
Decide which man (A-H) would be the most suitable for each woman (1-5).
For each of these numbers write the correct letter.

1. ☐ Mariana doesn't care whether her husband is handsome or rich. For her, the most important thing is to have a good family life. She enjoys cooking and looking after a household.

2. ☐ Silvia enjoys going to parties. She thinks it is important to impress her friends who are all very fashionable and sophisticated. She likes wearing expensive jewels and clothes.

3. ☐ Daniela is young and beautiful. She thinks that money is the most important thing in life. She loves gold more than people. But she cannot stand the thought of an old husband.

4. ☐ Francesca wants to be a nun but her parents insist that she marries. She wants a lot of time to herself for meditation and reading the Bible. She is afraid that she will be too busy for this if she is a wife.

5. ☐ Claudia has read a lot of romances. Her idea of a perfect husband is a man who adores his wife. She wants a man who will be her slave.

SINGLE MEN FROM VERONA

A Vincenzo has a great deal of gold and silver which he keeps in a secret place. People call him an old miser. He has decided to get married because he wants a young bride.

B Benedict has a lot of important friends and gets lots of invitations. He is very handsome and wears expensive clothes. He is looking for a wife who will not let him down when they are out together in society.

C His friends laugh at Dario because he treats women like goddesses. He believes that a man should serve his wife and try to fulfil all her dreams. He is young, handsome and well-educated.

D Paolo is a merchant who travels a great deal, so he is often away from home. He has enough servants, cooks and gardeners to look after everything in his house. His friends say that his wife will have nothing to do except wait for Paolo to come back from a journey.

E Carlo is not rich or handsome but he will make a very loving husband. He wants a wife who will stay at home and look after him. He does not want any children as he thinks his wife will pay him less attention if she becomes a mother.

F Rodrigo has always wanted to have a lot of children. He is only rich enough to have one servant, so he needs a wife who can help him care for his household. His female friends think that he is handsome but he says they are all too fond of pleasure to make a good wife for him.

G Inigo is very romantic. He showers his girlfriends with roses and hires musicians to serenade them at night. However, if he gets married, it is likely he will get bored with his wife and continue to flirt with the most beautiful women in Verona.

H Stefano is young and handsome. He has no money at the moment but his father is one of the richest men in Verona. The doctors expect his father to die soon, so Stefano, his only son, will inherit all his gold and property.

A Walk through Verona

Verona was born a very long time ago. In the year 100 AD it was already an important part of the Roman Empire. It became an important commercial, cultural and artistic centre because of its strategic [1] location. It was located at the crossroads of three important Roman roads.

Verona was built according to the typical Roman city plan. The Forum was always the civic, political and religious centre of a Roman city. In the medieval days, when Romeo and Juliet lived in Verona, the Forum had become Piazza Erbe. Piazza Erbe was, and still is, the heart of the city centre.

The powerful Scaligeri family ruled Verona for more than a century, from 1259 to 1387.

The famous 'Juliet's Balcony' in Verona.

Cangrande I della Scala was responsible for the great cultural and artistic development of Verona. The symbol of the Scaligeri was a ladder, as in the surname 'della Scala'. This symbol is still visible on many monuments.

During the Renaissance, the important families of Verona decorated the outside walls of their splendid homes and palaces with enormous paintings, called frescos. These families loved their city and wanted to make it as beautiful as possible.

1. **strategic** : most useful.

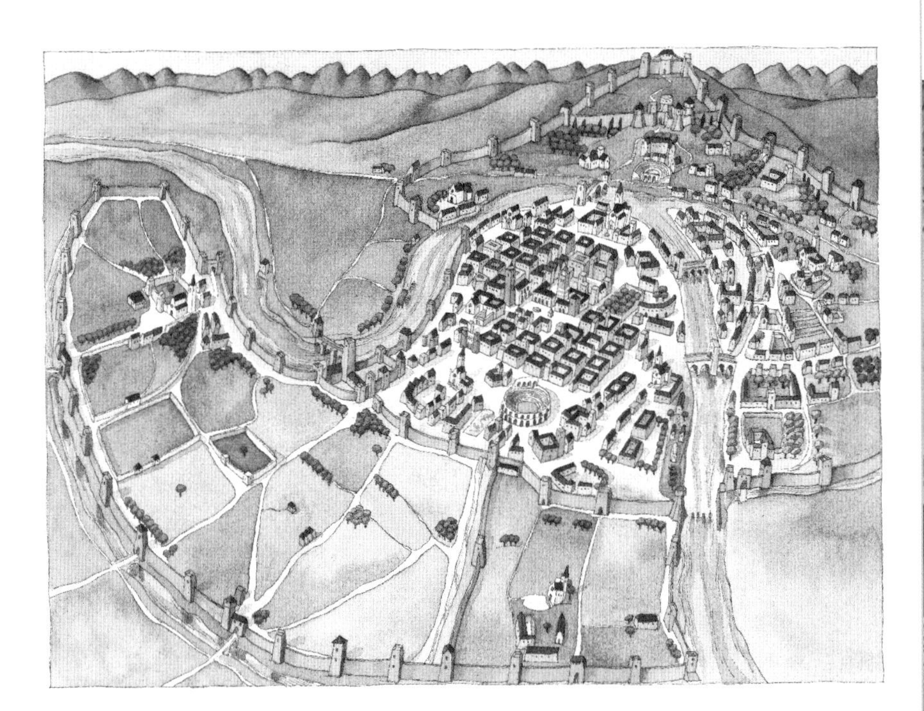

A map of the historical sites of Verona.

The Church of San Zeno, a splendid example of Romanesque architecture, was part of Romeo and Juliet's time. The huge Roman Amphitheatre, called the Arena, still remains in its original site. The medieval city grew around Piazza Erbe and the Arena.

Romeo and Juliet lived in the medieval centre of the city, near the Adige River. Juliet's house was in Via Cappello, a very busy street of medieval Verona. Lots of hat-makers and wine cask-makers [1] had their shops there. The famous balcony, where she and Romeo met at night, is in the courtyard of her home.

Romeo's house was behind the Scaligeri tombs, not far from Juliet's house.

Another important part of medieval Verona was the beautiful convent [2] of the

1. **wine cask-makers** : people who make wine casks. 
2. **convent** : the place where nuns live.

Franciscan Friars, where Romeo and Juliet were secretly married. Juliet's tomb is in the crypt [1] of the convent. Through the centuries, innumerable visitors such as Empress Maria Teresa of Austria, Charles Dickens and Lord Byron, have visited Juliet's tomb. People from all over the world, young and old, continue to visit Juliet's home, her tomb and her splendid city.

Juliet's tomb in the crypt of the Franciscan convent.

A view of Verona from the River Adige.

1. **crypt** : an underground room of a church.

PET 1 Read the text and the questions below. For each question, choose the correct answer, A, B, C or D.

1. Verona became an important commercial, cultural and artistic centre because

- **A** ☐ it was part of the Roman Empire
- **B** ☐ it won many wars
- **C** ☐ of its strategic location
- **D** ☐ it was connected by road to three other cities

2. According to the typical Roman city plan, the Forum was

- **A** ☐ an area for theatre and dance
- **B** ☐ the civic, political and religious centre
- **C** ☐ the main wall of the city
- **D** ☐ the main market place

3. Piazza Erbe is

- **A** ☐ the heart of the city centre
- **B** ☐ the religious centre of Verona
- **C** ☐ where Romeo and Juliet met
- **D** ☐ where Romeo and Juliet lived

4. Cangrande della Scala I, of the Scaligeri family,

- **A** ☐ was a bishop of the Church of San Zeno
- **B** ☐ was responsible for the great development of Verona
- **C** ☐ was a cruel Roman ruler
- **D** ☐ the ruler of Verona at the time of Shakespeare

5. Juliet's house was

- **A** ☐ in Via delle Arche Scaligere
- **B** ☐ near the Church of San Zeno
- **C** ☐ in Via Cappello
- **D** ☐ in an unknown location

6. Romeo and Juliet were secretly married

- **A** ☐ in the Church of San Zeno
- **B** ☐ in the convent of the Franciscan Friars
- **C** ☐ in Piazza Erbe
- **D** ☐ in a convent in a nearby city

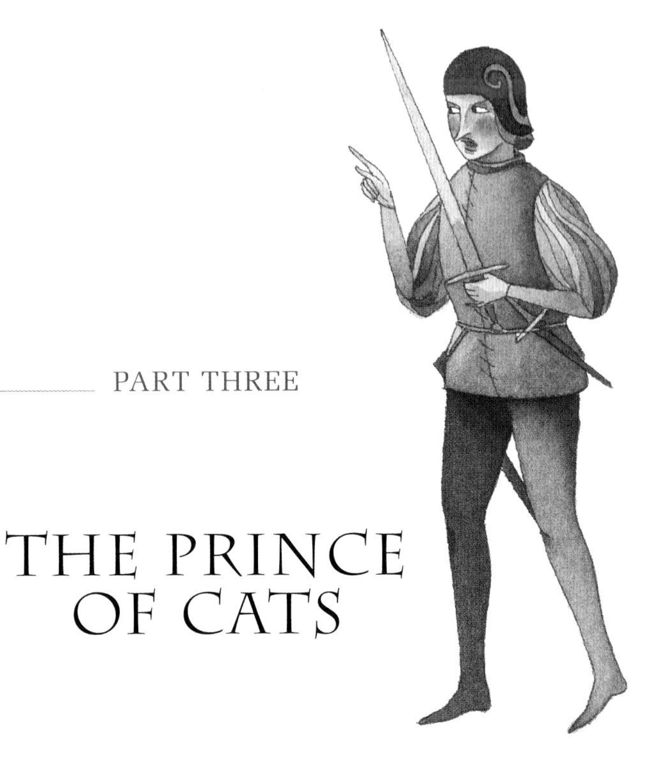

PART THREE

THE PRINCE OF CATS

Romeo went to see Friar [1] Laurence, his friend and teacher. The sun was rising and it was a beautiful morning. The Friar was working in his garden. He was an expert gardener who knew all the plants – the poisonous [2] ones, the medicinal [3] ones, the good and the bad ones.

'Friar,' said Romeo, 'I want to get married.'

'To Rosaline?' asked the Friar.

'No, I have forgotten Rosaline. She is nothing to me. I love Juliet and she loves me. You must help us. We want to get married today.'

'What? I see that young men's love is not in their hearts but in their eyes!'

1. **Friar** : a monk.

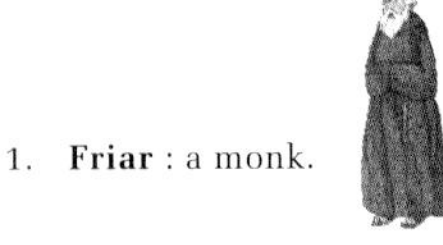

2. **poisonous** : it will kill you if you eat it.
3. **medicinal** : it can cure illnesses.

'But Friar, you often told me that I was foolish to love Rosaline. Juliet is my true love.'

'Well, perhaps your marriage will make the Capulets and the Montagues friends. It is a good thing for Verona. I will help you.'

Benvolio and Mercutio were looking for Romeo in the streets of Verona.

'Poor Romeo,' said Benvolio. 'His heart is broken. Rosaline does not love him.'

'That's not his only problem,' replied Mercutio. 'Tybalt has challenged [1] him. He has sent a letter to his house. He wants to fight him.'

'But Tybalt is dangerous.'

'Yes. Tybalt is the Prince of Cats. He is an artist with his sword. [2] Romeo is a lamb. [3] He will die.'

'Here comes Romeo.'

1. **challenged** : invited to fight.
2. **an artist with his sword** : he fights very well.
3. **a lamb** : a young sheep, an innocent person.

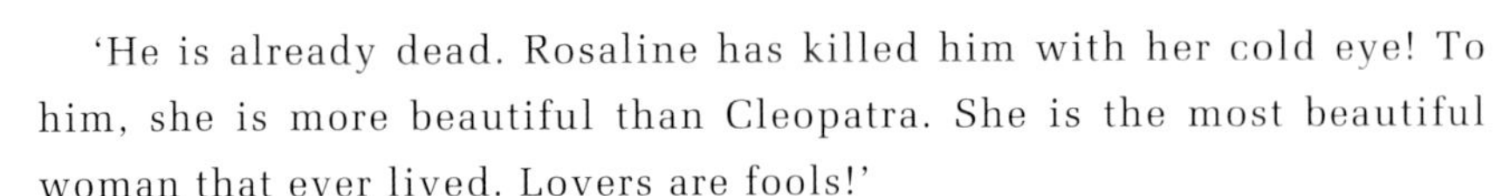

'He is already dead. Rosaline has killed him with her cold eye! To him, she is more beautiful than Cleopatra. She is the most beautiful woman that ever lived. Lovers are fools!'

Mercutio called to Romeo. 'Where did you go last night after the party? You ran away from us.'

'Excuse me. I was busy.'

'Busy with Rosaline, eh? Forget love, Romeo. Remember your friends. Friendship is more important than love.'

'But look,' said Mercutio, 'here comes a fat old woman.'

It was the Nurse. Juliet had sent her to find Romeo. 'I must speak alone with you, sir,' she said.

Mercutio laughed. 'Is this your new girlfriend?' he asked.

'Go away,' said Romeo. 'Now, Nurse, what do you want?'

'First of all, I want you to promise that you will be kind to Juliet. She is very young. You must not hurt her.'

'I love her.'

'Then what do you want me to tell her?'

'Tell Juliet to come to Friar Laurence's cell [1] this afternoon. We will get married there.'

'I love Juliet, sir. I

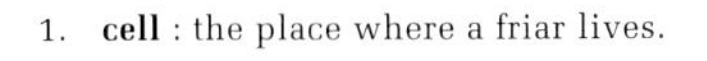

1. **cell** : the place where a friar lives.

remember when she was a little child. Look after her when you are her husband.'

The Nurse went back to Juliet who was waiting anxiously. She told her the news. 'Tell your parents that you are going to pray,' [1] said the Nurse. 'Then go to see Friar Laurence.'

The two lovers got ready [2] for their secret wedding.

In the afternoon, the sun was shining. Romeo went secretly to Friar Laurence's cell.

'The day is bright,' said the Friar. 'It is a sign that the future will be happy.'

'I do not care [3] if I die tomorrow. It is enough that Juliet is mine.'

'Don't be so passionate. It is better to love moderately. [4] Then love will last [5] longer.'

At last Juliet arrived. She was very nervous. So was Romeo. They were very young but very much in love. Friar Laurence was like a father to them. He took them into his cell and they were married.

Meanwhile, Benvolio and Mercutio were walking in the streets of Verona. 'Let's go home,' said Benvolio. 'The Capulets are out in the streets. If we meet them, we will have to fight. In this hot weather, young men do mad things.'

'Don't worry. We are safe.'

'Here come the Capulets. Tybalt is there!'

'The Prince of Cats. I am not afraid.'

1. **pray** : speak to God.
2. **got ready** : prepared themselves.
3. **I do not care** : it is not important to me.
4. **moderately** : not as great as desired.
5. **last** : endure, continue.

Tybalt approached Mercutio. 'I want to speak with you.'

'Do you want to speak or to fight?'

'You are not a Montague but a friend of Romeo. That makes you my enemy.'

'Be careful,' said Benvolio. 'We are in the public streets. If you fight, the Prince will be angry.'

At that moment, Romeo came back from his secret wedding.

'Fight, you villain!' [1] shouted Tybalt.

Romeo did not want to fight because Tybalt was Juliet's cousin. 'I am not a villain. But I will not fight with you.'

Mercutio was angry because he thought that Romeo was a coward. [2] He took out his own sword.

'What do you want?' asked Tybalt.

'I want one of your nine lives, Prince of Cats!'

'I will fight you as Romeo is too afraid to fight,' agreed Tybalt.

Romeo came between Mercutio and Tybalt as they began to fight. 'Stop fighting. The Prince will be angry. He will punish you. Stop fighting! Stop, Tybalt! Stop, good Mercutio!' shouted Romeo.

1. **villain** : a bad person.

2. **coward** : someone who is afraid.

But Tybalt took the opportunity to kill Mercutio. The sword passed under Romeo's arm as he stood between them. Then Tybalt ran quickly away.

Mercutio groaned. [1] 'Aaaaagh! I am hurt. I am dying. Romeo, this quarrel [2] between your families has killed me.'

'Are you badly hurt?' asked Romeo.

'A scratch, [3] a scratch. It's enough. Bring me a doctor.'

'Be brave, Mercutio. It cannot be so bad.'

'Look for me tomorrow in my grave. [4] The Prince of Cats has killed me. Why did you come between us?'

'I wanted to help...'

Mercutio fell to the ground and died. It was Romeo's fault. [5] His friend was dead.

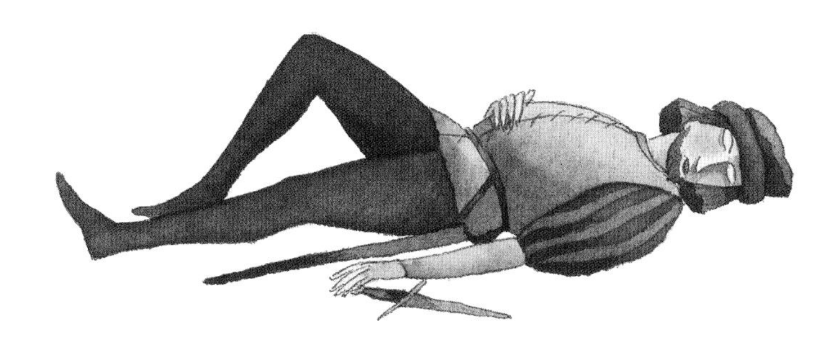

1. **groaned** : cried with pain.
2. **quarrel** : argument, fight.
3. **scratch** : a small wound; a cat can scratch you.
4. **grave** : the place for a dead person under the ground.
5. **fault** : mistake, responsibility.

Comprehension and Opinion

1 What happened in Part Three?

a. Why did Friar Laurence agree to help Romeo?
b. Who was the Prince of Cats?
c. What did Romeo tell the Nurse?
d. What happened at Friar Laurence's cell?
e. Why did Romeo refuse to fight Tybalt?
f. What was the result of the fight?

What do you think?

Mercutio said: 'Lovers are fools!' Do you agree?
Was Romeo responsible for his friend's death?

Animals and Character

2 Mercutio calls Tybalt 'the Prince of Cats' meaning that he is dangerous. He calls Romeo a 'lamb' meaning that he is gentle and innocent.
We often use animals when we are describing somebody figuratively.
Here are the names of some other creatures:

dog donkey fox horse lion mouse owl pig swan

Fill in the gaps below with the most suitable word from the list. Use one animal name twice.

He/She is

a. as brave as a ....
b. as dirty as a ....
c. as strong as a ....
d. as timid as a ....
e. as stupid as a ....

f. as clever as a ....

g. as faithful as a ....

h. as wise as an ....

i. as greedy as a ....

j. as beautiful as a ....

The Present Perfect（現在完成時）

Do you remember these sentences?

The Montagues and the Capulets have hated each other for hundreds of years.
Mercutio and Benvolio haven't seen Romeo since the party.

The verbs are in the Present Perfect tense. We use this tense when we are talking about a period of time between the PAST and NOW. We often use it with *for...* or *since...*

For example: *He **has lived** in Rome **for** sixteen years.*
*She **has lived** in Vienna **since** 1994.*

PET **3** **Here are some sentences about the characters in the story. For each question, complete the second sentence so that it means the same as the first, using no more than three words. Write the missing words in the gap.**

Example: I began to love Juliet when I first saw her.
I've loved Juliet since I first saw her.

1. Romeo began to be sad when he fell in love with Rosaline.
Romeo has .... he fell in love with Rosaline.

2. How long ago did Juliet meet Romeo?
How long .... Romeo? (use a form of *know*)

3. Juliet met Romeo twenty-four hours ago.
Juliet has .... twenty-four hours.

4. When did they begin to fight the Montagues?
How long .... the Montagues?

5. They began to fight them hundreds of years ago.
They have .... hundreds of years.

6. The Friar came here to live five years ago.
   The Friar has .... five years.
7. The Nurse began to tend Juliet when she was a baby.
   The Nurse has .... she was a baby.
8. The Nurse began to work for the Capulets at 15 years old.
   The Nurse has worked for the Capulets .... 15 years old.

The Nurse and Juliet

4 You will hear a conversation between Juliet and the Nurse. The Nurse has returned from the city where she has seen Romeo. Juliet wants to know the news but the Nurse makes her wait. Listen carefully. Write down Juliet's questions.

Juliet: Where [1] .... ?
Why [2] .... ? Ah, she's here.
Have [3] .... ?

Nurse: I am very tired. I have run from the town. My bones ache.[1]

Juliet: What [4] .... ?

Nurse: Well, I have seen Romeo. He is handsome, young and polite. But have you had dinner yet?

Juliet: Nurse, don't ask stupid questions.
What [5] .... ?

Nurse: My head aches. I am very tired.

Juliet: I am sorry for you.
But sweet Nurse, what [6] .... ?

Nurse: He says... Where is your mother?

Juliet: She's in the house. But please be quick.
Is [7] .... ?

Nurse: Don't be angry. I have run all over the city for you. Next time, go and ask Romeo yourself.

Juliet: Sweet Nurse, please tell me.
Did [8] .... ?

Nurse: He wants to marry you at Friar Laurence's cell this afternoon.

Juliet: Aaah! Thank you, Nurse.

1. **ache** : hurt, cause pain.

5 **Look at these pictures. They tell the story of Parts One, Two and Three of *Romeo and Juliet.***

1. fight

2. tell

3. decide

4. go

5. see

6. kiss

7. jump

8. talk

9. meet

10. get married

11. fight

12. die

What are the Past Simple forms of the verbs below the pictures?

1.	fight	fought	**7.**	jump	....
2.	tell	....	**8.**	talk	....
3.	decide	....	**9.**	meet	....
4.	go	....	**10.**	get	....
5.	see	....	**11.**	fight	....
6.	kiss	....	**12.**	die	....

Now write your summary of the action. Put the verbs in the past tense and use the linking words to join some of them.
Begin:

The Montagues and the Capulets hated each other.
One day they fought in the streets...

But then **2.** .... *Later,*
3. ....
4. ....
At the party, **5.** ....
and **6.** ....
After the party, **7.** ....
8. ....*and, next day,*
9. ....
In the afternoon, **10.** ....
But in the city streets, **11.** ....
12. ....

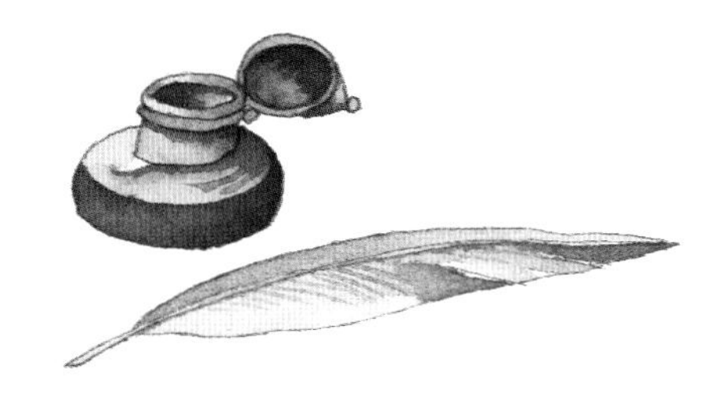

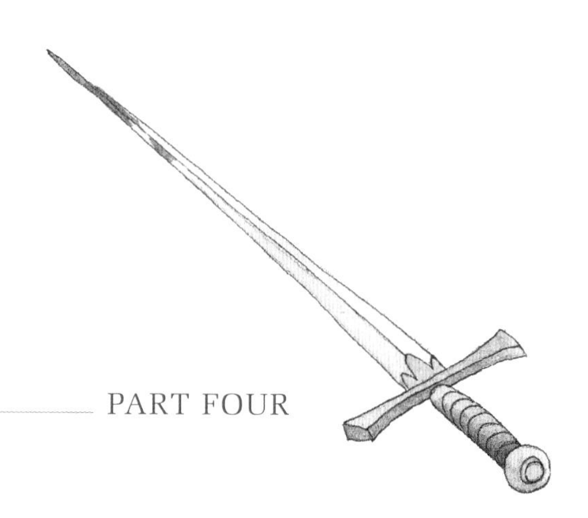

PART FOUR

FORTUNE'S FOOL[1]

At that moment, Tybalt returned.

'Boy!' shouted Tybalt. 'You came here with Mercutio and you will die as he did!'

Romeo was so angry that he lost control. He took out his sword and fought with Tybalt. He killed him.

'He killed my friend. Now he is dead. He is with Mercutio. Juliet, your love made me a coward but now I am brave.'

Benvolio took his arm. 'Romeo, you must escape. The people are coming. The Prince will punish you with death.'[2]

'Oh, I am Fortune's fool!' With those words, Romeo ran away.

Soon, the citizens arrived, followed by the Prince. They saw Mercutio and Tybalt lying dead on the ground.

1. **Fortune's Fool** : the victim of bad luck, of Fate.
2. **punish you with death** : Benvolio thinks the Prince will kill Romeo because he has killed Tybalt.

'Where are the people who began this fight?' asked the Prince angrily.

'I can tell you the complete story,' promised Benvolio.

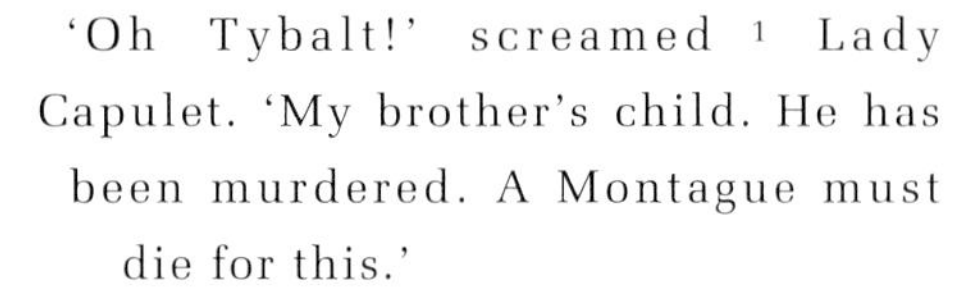

'Oh Tybalt!' screamed [1] Lady Capulet. 'My brother's child. He has been murdered. A Montague must die for this.'

'Romeo wanted to stop the fight,' explained Benvolio. 'But Tybalt killed Mercutio. Then Romeo killed Tybalt.'

'He is lying!' [2] said Lady Capulet. 'He is a Montague. Romeo killed Tybalt. So Romeo must not live.'

'Romeo killed Tybalt. But Tybalt killed Mercutio,' said the Prince.

'Mercutio was Romeo's friend,' agreed Lord Montague. 'Romeo was right to kill his friend's killer.'

The Prince spoke seriously. 'No! It is wrong to kill. We banish [3] Romeo from Verona! If I find him in the city, he will die! We must not show mercy [4] to murderers.'

Those were the Prince's final words. Romeo had to leave Verona and never return.

Juliet was waiting for Romeo, her new husband. She wanted the night to come quickly so that they could be together. But when the Nurse arrived, she brought bad news.

1. **screamed** : shouted in a high voice.
2. **lying** : not telling the truth.
3. **banish** : send away from the city, exile.
4. **mercy** : pity, forgiveness.

'He is dead!'

'Who is dead?'

'I saw the body with my own eyes. He is dead.'

'What? Is Romeo dead?'

'No, Tybalt is dead. Romeo has killed him. Romeo is banished, he must leave Verona.'

'Did Romeo kill my cousin? He is a villain. But I love him.'

Juliet was very unhappy. 'Your father and mother are crying for Tybalt,' the Nurse told her.

'I will cry for him too,' said Juliet. 'But I will cry longer for Romeo. I will never see him again. I will kill myself.'

'No,' said the Nurse. 'Romeo is hiding [1] with Friar Laurence. I will bring him to you.'

'Yes, Nurse, bring him to me quickly. Give him this ring. He must come and say his last goodbye.'

Romeo was talking to Friar Laurence. 'Everything is finished. I must leave Verona and never see Juliet again. Even a cat or a dog or a mouse may look at Juliet. But I cannot. Give me poison or a knife to kill myself.'

'You are mad. The Prince has shown mercy. He lets you live.'

'You are old, Friar. But I am young and in love. I want to die.'

1. **hiding** : staying in a secret place.

'No, be brave. You must go to Mantua. You will be safe there. I will send you news about Juliet. One day, you will be together again. But here is the Nurse.'

'How is Juliet?' Romeo asked her immediately.

'She cries and cries. First, she calls out Tybalt's name, then she calls for Romeo. Then she falls on her bed.'

'Tonight, go with the Nurse,' said the Friar. 'See Juliet for the last time.'

Romeo went back to the house of the Capulets. The Nurse took him into the garden. Nobody saw them.

'Here is a ladder,' [1] she said. 'Climb up and go through the window.'

So Romeo spent his marriage night with Juliet.

Downstairs, in the house of the Capulets, Lord and Lady Capulet were talking. Lord Paris was with them.

'I will talk to Juliet. She will marry you next Wednesday...'

'That's too soon,' said Lady Capulet.

'On Thursday then. Tybalt is dead. There must be something good for the Capulet family – Juliet's wedding! I am her father. She will do as I say.'

Paris was very happy because he loved Juliet. Lord Capulet told his wife to see Juliet

1. **ladder** : 

in the morning. She must prepare for her marriage. Her parents did not know that Juliet was already married to Romeo, the killer of her cousin Tybalt.

'I wish it was Thursday tomorrow,' said Paris.

'Well, goodbye until then,' said Lord Capulet. 'On Thursday, my daughter will marry you. I promise.'

In the morning, Romeo left Juliet. He had to escape to Mantua before the Prince found him.

'Must you go?' asked Juliet. 'It is still night. The nightingale [1] is singing, not the lark.' [2]

'Look at the sky. The sun is rising. But I want to stay.'

'Go. It is dangerous for you here. But I want you to stay. Goodbye, sweet Romeo. Will I ever see you again?'

'Goodbye. I will think of you every second of the day.'

They kissed. Then Romeo climbed down the ladder.

'I can see only bad luck in the future,' said Juliet. 'I seem to see you dead.'

'Our sadness makes us think in this way. I will write every day. Goodbye.'

'Please, God, send him back to me again.'

1. **the nightingale** : a night bird.
2. **the lark** : a morning bird.

Comprehension and Opinion

1 What happened in Part Four?

a. Why did Romeo fight with Tybalt?
b. What did the Prince decide?
c. Did Juliet hate Romeo for killing Tybalt?
d. Where did Romeo have to go?
e. Why was Paris happy?
f. Why was Juliet sad?

What do you think?

Was Romeo right to kill Tybalt? What should Juliet do?

Word Formation

2 Look at these words:

lucky luckier luckiest luckily unluckily
unlucky unluckier unluckiest luck

All these words come from the word 'luck'. Put one suitable word from the list in each gap in the sentences below. You can use the same word more than once.

a. Romeo and Juliet are the .... lovers in history.
b. Mercutio had very bad ....
c. ...., the Prince did not find Romeo.
d. If Romeo has good ...., he will see Juliet again.
e. Romeo is not very ....
f. It was .... that Romeo and Juliet came from families which were enemies.
g. During their fight, Tybalt was .... than Mercutio.
h. ...., Tybalt recognised Romeo at the party.
i. Before he left, Benvolio said, 'Good ....' to Romeo.
j. 'I will be the .... man in the world if you marry me,' said Romeo.

How many words can you make from:

fortune succeed fail die friend love marry

T: GRADE 5

3 TOPIC – CUSTOMS AND BELIEFS
Show an object to your friend(s). You think the object brings you good luck. Think about the following questions:

a. When and where did you get the lucky charm from?
b. Has it brought you luck yet? When?
c. What other things in your country are considered lucky and unlucky?
d. Think about a wedding, what things are considered lucky and unlucky?

Already, *Still* and *Yet*

4 Look at these sentences about the story:

Juliet has ***already*** *married Romeo.*
Lord Capulet ***still*** *wants Paris to marry Juliet.*
Romeo hasn't gone to Mantua ***yet****.*

Here are some short stories. Put *already* or *yet* or *still* in the gaps in the stories.

a. Susan expects to marry David. She has .... bought a wedding dress and invited a hundred guests. But David .... loves his old girlfriend, Julia. He hasn't forgotten her ....
b. It is .... January but Bill has .... sent a Valentine's card to his sweetheart, Rose. She hasn't sent him his Christmas present .... for last year. But he .... loves her.
c. Simon loves eating Italian food. This morning, he has .... eaten three dishes of pasta. He is .... hungry. 'Haven't you cooked dinner ....?' he asks his mother. 'No, I'm .... washing the dishes,' she answers.
d. Ben is going on holiday to Verona. He has .... been there six times. He loves the city because it is the city of Romeo and Juliet. 'Their ghosts haven't gone away ....,' he believes. 'They are .... talking together in the moonlit garden.'

Four Zodiac[1] Signs

PET 5 **You will hear someone talking about horoscopes.[2] For each question, put a tick (✓) in the correct box.**

9

1. Capricorns will
   - **A** ☐ be very successful in love.
   - **B** ☐ fall in love.
   - **C** ☐ travel to interesting places in this country.

2. Cancers will have
   - **A** ☐ a similar social life to Capricorns.
   - **B** ☐ a worse social life than Capricorns.
   - **C** ☐ a much better social life than Capricorns.

3. For Leos, it will be a good year for
   - **A** ☐ love and social life.
   - **B** ☐ work and travel.
   - **C** ☐ love and health.

4. There will be broken hearts
   - **A** ☐ for Librans born after the new moon.
   - **B** ☐ for all Librans.
   - **C** ☐ for some Librans.

5. In general, Librans may well have
   - **A** ☐ a bad year.
   - **B** ☐ a good year.
   - **C** ☐ a bad first half of the year.

6. The horoscopes include predictions about
   - **A** ☐ marriage, social life and travel.
   - **B** ☐ work, love and money.
   - **C** ☐ work, love and social life.

1. **zodiac** : an area of the sky divided into 12 equal parts.
2. **horoscopes** : telling one's future based on the position of the stars when one is born.

PET **6** **This is part of a letter you have received from an English penfriend.**

In your last letter, you said that you have had a lucky year. Please tell me all about your good luck next time you write.

Now you are replying to this letter.
Write your letter in about 100 words.

....
....
....
....
....
....
....
....

7 **Someone has asked you to write a short article for a student magazine about superstitions [1] in your country.**
Your article must begin with this sentence:

In my country there are some things that people think are lucky and others which they think are unlucky.

Write your article in about 100 words.

....
....
....
....
....
....
....
....

1. **superstitions** : beliefs that certain events cannot be explained by human reason.

Life in Renaissance Verona

During the Renaissance, social class and dress were closely related. Rich families had beautiful clothes made for them. Silk, satin, brocade, [1] gold, and precious jewels were used for the clothes of important men, women and children.

Wealthy men and boys wore coloured leggings [2] and elaborate shirts, jackets and mantles. [3] They also wore hats with coloured feathers. Often, the colours of the clothes were those of the family coat of arms. [4]

Young girls and women of rich families wore dresses that were very ornamental. These dresses were decorated with precious stones, pearls, gold and silver threads. It usually took many years to make a dress! Several servants and tailors worked on only one dress.

The poor dressed with simple clothes of wool or cotton, with no decoration.

Young boys and men wore a dagger [5] on their belt for protection. Some also carried a sword. Family feuds [6] were common in those days, and there were often street fights.

Alessandro Farnese (*c*. 1561) by Sofonisba Anguissola.

1. **brocade** : cloth with a raised pattern of gold or silver threads.
2. **leggings** :
3. **mantles** : loose, sleeveless cloak.
4. **coat of arms** :
5. **dagger** :
6. **feuds** : hatred or violence which continues over a long period of time, between people or families.

A horse was a status symbol. Only the members of important families rode a horse. The others went on foot.
The upper classes often gave costume balls in the dance halls of their enormous homes and palaces. Only those who were invited could go to the ball.
Things have certainly changed in our times. Men and women, rich and poor, usually dress in a similar way. Many clothes are unisex. We don't have our clothes made by hand. We buy them in shops.

Portrait of a young woman: Antea (second half of the 16th century) by Parmigianino.

Today we don't carry daggers or swords. Most young people have a means of transportation – either a bicycle, a scooter, [1] a motorbike or a car. We don't need a special invitation to go dancing. We simply go to a disco, whenever we want.

However, one habit has remained the same: the late afternoon walk in the main road or square. Just as Romeo and his friends met in the main square of Verona, our young people do the same. They meet, take a walk and talk in the main road or square of their city or town.

PET

1 For each question, mark the letter next to the correct answer.

1. During the Renaissance, clothes often indicated all of these except:

A ☐ social class.
B ☐ wealth.
C ☐ marriage status: single or married.
D ☐ family.

2. What did rich men and boys often wear?

A ☐ The same kind of clothes as women.
B ☐ Beautiful, elaborate clothes.
C ☐ Hats made of feathers.
D ☐ Coats of arms.

3. It is not true that normally

A ☐ it took years to make a dress.
B ☐ it took many people to make a dress.
C ☐ dresses had a lot of expensive decoration.
D ☐ dresses were made of wool or cotton.

1. **scooter** : a light motor-cycle.

4. What did all men and boys do?

A ☐ They carried swords and daggers.

B ☐ They carried daggers.

C ☐ They carried daggers and rode horses.

D ☐ They gave costume balls in their dance halls.

5. Which of the following is the best description of the whole text?

A ☐ Information about the way that people lived in Renaissance Verona.

B ☐ A comparison of life in Renaissance Verona and now.

C ☐ A description of people's clothes in Renaissance Verona.

D ☐ Information about the different classes in Renaissance Verona.

Word Puzzle

2 Find the word in the text to match these descriptions:

a. a soft, shiny cloth : _ _ _ _

b. a precious stone : _ _ _ _ _

c. a person who makes clothes : _ _ _ _ _ _

d. a type of knife : _ _ _ _ _ _

e. a big, formal dance : _ _ _ _

f. an old means of transportation : _ _ _ _ _

g. clothes that both men and women wear : _ _ _ _ _ _

PART FIVE

MY LADY'S DEAD!

arly next morning, Lady Capulet visited Juliet in her bedroom. 'Daughter, are you awake?'

'It is very early. I am not well,' answered Juliet.

'Are you still crying for your cousin Tybalt? It is good to cry. But now it is time to stop.'

'Let me cry more for my poor cousin.'

'Well, really you should cry because Romeo, his killer, is still alive.'

'Yes, mother. I wish I could see Romeo now and... kill him.'

'I will send a servant to Mantua to poison him,' promised Lady Capulet. 'He will not live long. But Juliet, I have good news for you. You will get married to Paris early next Thursday morning. Then you will be happy.'

'No, mother. It is impossible. I don't want to get married so soon. Tell my father this. As you know, I hate Romeo. He has killed my

cousin. But I'd rather [1] marry Romeo than Paris.'

'Here comes your father. Tell him yourself.'

'What?' said Lord Capulet. 'Are you still crying? Wife, have you told her the news?'

'Yes. The little fool thanks you but she won't marry Paris.'

Lord Capulet was very angry. 'Lord Paris is a very fine gentleman. This is a great opportunity.'

'Thank you, father, but I will not marry him.'

'Are you too proud [2] to marry him? Put on a wedding dress next Thursday and go with Paris to the church. If you don't, I'll pull you there by the hair.'

'Good father, listen to me.'

'Don't argue [3] with me. Go to the church next Thursday. I'm glad we have no more children like this.'

1. **I'd rather** : I would prefer to.
2. **are you too proud** : (here) do you think you are too superior?
3. **argue** : disagree.

'Please don't be angry with my little Juliet, sir,' said the Nurse.

'Shut up, you fat old fool!'

'Be calm,' Lady Capulet told him.

'I have decided. If you don't obey me, [1] I will throw you out in the street.'

When her parents had gone, Juliet asked the Nurse for advice. [2]

'I already have a husband that I love. What should I do?'

'Well, Romeo is not here. Paris is a fine gentleman, it's true. He is more handsome than Romeo. Forget Romeo and marry Paris.'

'Do you speak from your heart?'

'Of course,' said the Nurse.

Juliet realised that she could not trust [3] the Nurse. She went to Friar Laurence to ask his advice.

The Friar was very worried. Paris was talking to him and had told him that he would marry Juliet.

'Does she love you?' asked the Friar.

'I don't know. We haven't talked about love because she is weeping [4] for her cousin's death. But our marriage will make her happy again.'

'But look, here comes Juliet.'

'Welcome, my lady and my wife,' said Paris. 'Have you come to tell the Friar that you love me?'

'I cannot answer that,' said Juliet. 'But please, let me talk to the Friar privately.'

When they were alone, the Friar told Juliet to be happy. 'If you are brave enough, I have a plan that will help you and Romeo. You will be together again.'

'What must I do? I will do anything for Romeo, my husband.'

'Go home and agree to marry Paris.'

1. **obey me** : follow my instructions, do as I say.
2. **advice** : help, guidance.
3. **trust** : believe in, be friendly with.
4. **weeping** : crying.

'No! I cannot.'

'Listen carefully. On Wednesday night, go to your bedroom alone. Take this bottle and drink the liquid. It is a special potion. [1] You will sleep for forty-two hours. Your family will think that you are dead. They will carry you to the tomb [2] of the Capulets. Meanwhile, I will send a message to Romeo. He will come secretly to the tomb. When you wake up, you can escape together. Are you brave enough to do this, Juliet?'

'Give me the bottle, Friar. Love will give me strength.'

Juliet went home. Lord and Lady Capulet were very happy when she told them that she had met Paris at Friar Laurence's cell and that she would marry him.

'Now I am going to my room to pray. Do not come with me, Nurse, I want to be alone.'

In her room, Juliet looked at the bottle of mysterious liquid which Friar Laurence had given her.

'I am afraid. Perhaps it is poison. Or perhaps I will wake in the tomb and Romeo will not be there. I will be alone in the middle of all the dead bodies with my dead cousin, Tybalt. It will be terrible.'

Bravely, [3] Juliet picked up the bottle and raised it to her lips.

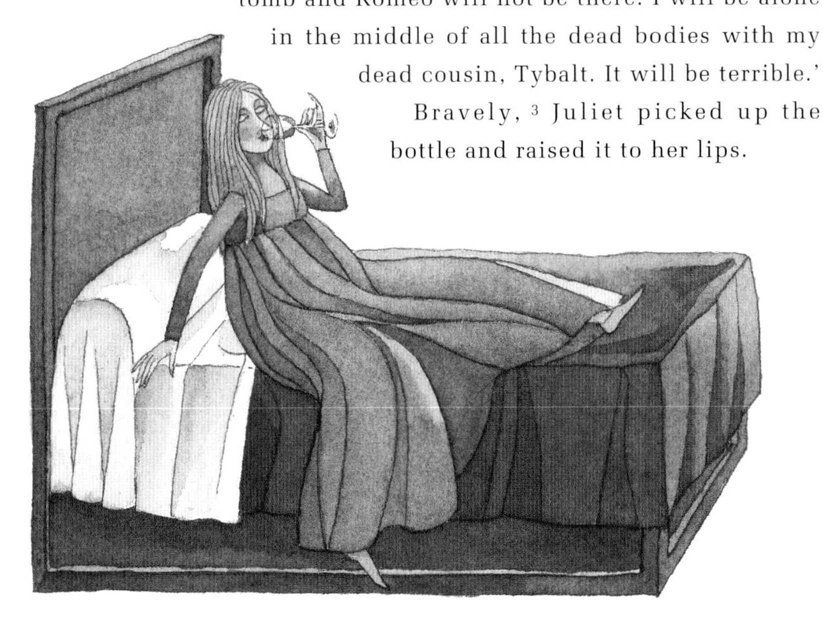

1. **potion** : a drink with a special effect.
2. **tomb** : a place to put dead people.
3. **bravely** : without fear.

'Romeo, Romeo, I drink to you!'

She drank. She fell on the bed and slept.

The next morning, it was Thursday. The Nurse came to wake her up for her marriage. 'You lazy girl,' she said. 'You mustn't lie in bed on your wedding day... Help! Help! My lady's dead!'

Lord and Lady Capulet ran to their daughter's room.

'She's dead, she's dead, she's dead,' cried Lady Capulet.

'Her body is cold. I cannot speak,' said Lord Capulet.

At that moment, Paris and Friar Laurence entered the house. 'Is Juliet ready to go to the church?' asked the Friar.

'Oh Paris,' said Lord Capulet, 'death has taken your wife.'

The Nurse began to cry. 'O terrible day! O sad day! O horrible day! There has never been such a black day. O sad day! O unhappy day!'

'Do not be sad,' said the Friar. 'Juliet is in Heaven. She is happier there than when she was alive.'

'The wedding must become a funeral,' [1] said Lord Capulet. 'Tell the musicians to play sad tunes. [2] Put the wedding flowers on my daughter's body.'

Lord and Lady Capulet took Juliet to the tomb of the Capulets. The Nurse, Lord Paris and Friar Laurence followed her body. The Friar was the only one who knew the secret – Juliet was alive. He was thinking: 'I have sent Friar John to Mantua to tell Romeo to come back to Verona. He will be here when Juliet wakes up.'

1. **funeral** : a ceremony for burying a dead person.
2. **tunes** : music.

Comprehension and Opinion

1 What happened in Part Five?

- **a.** What did Lady Capulet tell Juliet?
- **b.** What did Lord Capulet say he would do to Juliet?
- **c.** What did the Nurse tell Juliet to do?
- **d.** How long would Juliet sleep after drinking the liquid?
- **e.** What did Juliet say as she drank the liquid?
- **f.** Why had Friar John gone to Mantua?

What do you think?

Will the Friar's plan succeed?
What will happen if Friar John doesn't reach Mantua in time?

Past Perfect (過去完成時) versus Past Simple (過去時)

Look at this sentence:

*After Romeo **had met** the servant, he **went** to the party.*

There are two actions in the past – 'had met' and 'went'. We use the Past Perfect form for the earlier action: *had met* and the Past Simple for the later action: *went*

2 In each sentence below, put one of the verbs in the Past Perfect and one in the Past Simple.

- **a.** Romeo .... *(be)* in love with Rosaline before he .... *(see)* Juliet.
- **b.** After he .... *(hear)* her speaking on her balcony, he .... *(know)* that she loved him.

c. Tybalt .... *(challenge)* Romeo to fight because he .... *(go)* to the Capulets' party.

d. After Tybalt .... *(kill)* Mercutio, Romeo .... *(lose)* control.

e. The Prince .... *(send)* Romeo away because he .... *(kill)* Tybalt.

f. Paris .... *(not know)* that Juliet .... *(marry)* Romeo.

g. Although the Nurse .... *(help)* Romeo, later she .... *(tell)* Juliet to marry Paris.

h. Juliet .... *(drink)* from the bottle that the Friar .... *(give)* her.

i. After she .... *(drink)* the liquid, she .... *(fall)* asleep.

j. The Nurse .... *(think)* that Juliet was asleep but then she .... *(think)* that she was dead.

PET **3** **Look at the text in each question. What does it say?**
Mark the letter next to the correct explanation – A, B or C.

Example:

NO STREET
FIGHTS
AT ANY TIME

A ☑ You must never fight in the streets.
B ☐ You can fight in the streets sometimes.
C ☐ You can fight but not in the streets.

1.

POISONOUS LIQUID
KEEP AWAY
FROM CHILDREN!!!

A ☐ Adults but not children may drink this.
B ☐ Only drink this when you are far away from children.
C ☐ You shouldn't let children have access to this liquid.

2. Guests for the wedding of
Juliet Capulet and Lord Paris
should be at the church by noon.

A ☐ No guests should arrive before noon.
B ☐ The wedding will start at noon or soon afterwards.
C ☐ The wedding will be finished before noon.

3. Come to the convent
within an hour of
receiving this message.

A ☐ You should come to the convent soon after you get this message.
B ☐ You should wait for an hour before coming to the convent.
C ☐ You can come to the convent at any time.

4. e-mail:
To: Friar John@saintmarks
From: Friar Laurence
Cancel your journey to Padua tomorrow and
start for Mantua today to warn Romeo.

Friar John should
A ☐ go to Mantua today and Padua tomorrow.
B ☐ start his journey from Mantua.
C ☐ change the date and destination of his journey.

5. DANGER!!!
THIS AREA IS CLOSED
TO THE PUBLIC
FOR AT LEAST FOUR WEEKS
BECAUSE OF THE RISK OF PLAGUE.

A ☐ The area will be safe after four weeks.
B ☐ You cannot enter this area.
C ☐ Be careful: if you enter this area, you may catch the plague.

Parents and Children

4 **Juliet's parents wanted to make her marry Paris. What should parents decide for their children? Fill in the table below to show what you think. Put a cross (✗) for 'NO' and a tick (✓) for 'YES'.**

PARENTS SHOULD DECIDE:

	age of child in years	**9-10**	**11-12**	**13-14**	**15-16**
a.	the time they come home at night:	☐	☐	☐	☐
b.	the TV programmes they watch:	☐	☐	☐	☐
c.	the time they go to bed:	☐	☐	☐	☐
d.	the time they spend on homework:	☐	☐	☐	☐
e.	where they go on holiday:	☐	☐	☐	☐
f.	the kind of clothes they wear:	☐	☐	☐	☐
g.	the friends they go out with:	☐	☐	☐	☐

Discuss your answers with your friend(s).

T: GRADE 5

5 **TOPIC – ENTERTAINMENT**
Bring a programme or advertisement for the cinema, television or a club that you know.
Talk about the following:

a. Tell your friend(s) about the club or film that you know or talk about which programmes you like to watch on television.

b. What things do other young people like doing in their free time in your town?

c. Do your parents tell you what you should and shouldn't do in their free time? Give examples.

6 **This is part of a letter that you receive from a friend in another country.**

In my country, anyone under 21 can't marry without the agreement of his or her parents. You cannot get a driving licence or drink alcohol until you're 20. What rights do teenagers have in your country?

Now you are replying to this letter.
Write your letter in about 100 words.

....
....
....
....
....
....
....
....
....
....
....
....
....
....

True or False

11 **7** **You will hear twelve statements about the story repeated twice. ELEVEN of them are not completely true. For each one, write down the truth.**

For example, if you hear: *Romeo was Mercutio's brother.*

write: Romeo was Mercutio's **friend**.

Be careful! ONE of the statements is true.

1. ....

2. ....

3. ....

4. ....

5. ....
6. ....
7. ....
8. ....
9. ....
10. ....
11. ....
12. ....

The Verona Times

8 **This is part of a letter that Benvolio received from the editor of the *Verona Times*.**

We have heard about the death of Juliet Capulet. Please send us a report about her death.

Now you are replying to this letter. Write your letter in about 100 words.

OR The editor of the *Verona Times* has asked you to write a report about the day that Mercutio and Tybalt died. Your report must begin with this sentence:

This morning the violent deaths of two rich young men occurred in Verona.

Write your report in about 100 words.

PART SIX

WITH A KISS, I DIE

Romeo was in the city of Mantua.

'I have been dreaming about Juliet. I was dead but when she kissed me I became a king. Even a dream of love is sweet. This dream has made me happy.'

At that moment, his servant Balthasar, found him. He had come with the latest news from Verona.

'Balthasar! What is the news from Verona? Have you got letters from the Friar? How is my mother? How is my father? How is Juliet?'

His servant replied sadly. 'Juliet is dead. She lies in the tomb of the Capulets.'

'What! Get me some horses. I will ride to Verona tonight.'

When Balthasar had gone, Romeo made his plans. 'I will go to the tomb. I will kiss her for the last time. Then I will drink poison. If Juliet is dead, I will die too.' He began to think carefully. 'There is an apothecary [1] who has a shop near here. He is very poor. If I pay him well, he will sell me some poison.'

So Romeo went to the apothecary and gave him some gold.

'Here is the poison. It is enough to kill twenty men.'

In the middle of the night, Paris was at the tomb of the Capulets. He had come to put flowers on Juliet's grave.

'Sweet Juliet,' said Paris, 'I will visit your grave every night and cry for you. But someone is coming. I will hide and watch...'

Romeo arrived at the tomb with his servant. 'Give this letter to my father tomorrow morning, Balthasar. Now go away. Don't try to stop me. I am stronger than tigers or the roaring [2] sea.'

Romeo used a strong metal bar to open the tomb. Paris was watching. 'This is Romeo, who murdered Juliet's cousin. He has come here to damage the tomb. I will arrest him!'

Paris called to Romeo. 'You are a Montague, the one who killed Tybalt. You must die!'

'I do not know you,' said Romeo. 'Go away if you want to live. Do not fight with me. I am desperate.' [3]

'I arrest you, murderer!' said Paris.

They began to fight.

Romeo fought like a madman. He was stronger than Paris and killed him.

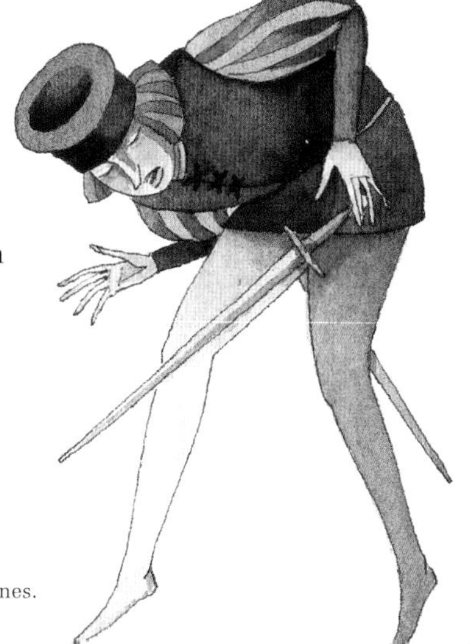

1. **apothecary** : a pharmacist, a person who sells medicines.
2. **roaring** : making a great sound, like a lion or tiger.
3. **desperate** : having no hope and ready to do anything.

'Put my body with Juliet,' cried Paris as he died.

Romeo knelt down [1] to look at his face.

'It is Paris! Balthasar told me that he wanted to marry Juliet. We are both unlucky. But where is Juliet? I must look at her beauty for the last time.'

Romeo went inside the tomb. He saw Juliet lying there and thought that she was dead.

'Oh my love, my wife! Death has kissed you. But you are still beautiful. Death is jealous. He keeps [2] you here as his lover. I will also stay here. But let me hold you in my arms. I love you.'

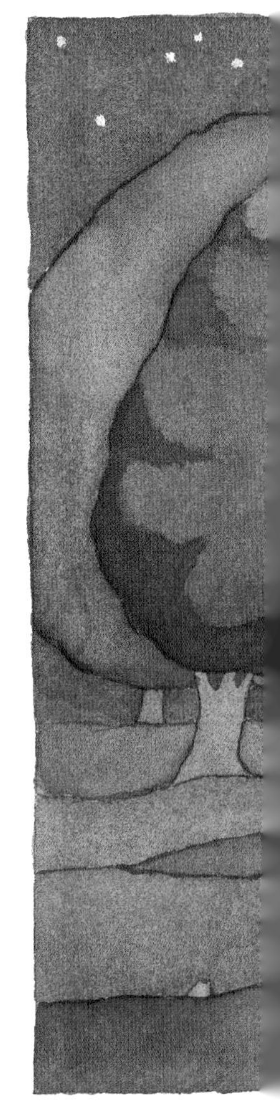

Romeo held Juliet. He took a cup of poison out of his pocket and raised it to his lips.

Outside, someone was calling him: 'Romeo! Romeo!'

He kissed Juliet. 'With a kiss, I die.'

Meanwhile, Friar John had come to Friar Laurence's cell.

'Have you given my letter to Romeo, Friar John?'

'No, Friar Laurence. I did not reach [3] Mantua. There was plague [4] in one of the villages on the road and the soldiers did not let me pass.'

'What! This is bad news. If Juliet wakes when Romeo is not there, she will be afraid. I must go to her.'

Friar Laurence hurried [5] to the tomb. He met Balthasar.

'I can see a light in the tomb. Who is looking among the skulls [6] and the worms?' [7]

'It is my master, Romeo.'

'How long has he been there?'

1. **knelt down** : went down on his knees.
2. **keeps** : holds.
3. **reach** : arrive at.
4. **plague** : a very serious illness that spreads quickly.
5. **hurried** : went quickly.
6. **skull** : hard bone of the head.

7. **worms** : small animals with a long, thin body, no bones and no legs.

'Half an hour. I was sleeping but I dreamt there was a fight between my master and another man.'

'I must go to him. Romeo! Romeo!'

But when the Friar went inside the tomb, Romeo had already drunk the poison. He was dead.

Inside the tomb, it was cold and dark. Juliet woke up and saw the Friar.

'Where is Romeo?' she asked.

'He is dead,' replied the Friar. 'Paris is also dead. But we must go. The Watchman [1] is coming. Come with me. I will take you to the nuns [2] who will let you live with them.'

'No, I will stay with Romeo,' said Juliet.

The Friar left her. Juliet held Romeo in her arms.

'I will drink poison too – but the cup is empty. Let me kiss his lips. They are still warm. But I can hear people coming.'

Outside the tomb, the Watchman was approaching.

'Quick, here is Romeo's dagger. Let me die!'

Juliet stabbed [3] herself and fell.

Everyone arrived at the tomb of the Capulets. It was too late. Romeo and Juliet had both died. Their great love story was finished.

'Here is the body of Paris,' said the Watchman. 'And here are the bodies of a boy and girl.'

'Juliet!' cried Lord Capulet. 'There is blood and a dagger. Our only daughter is dead. This is a terrible day for the Capulets.'

Lord Montague spoke: 'Last night, my wife died from a broken heart because Romeo was banished from Verona. Now *he* is dead, poisoned. This is a terrible day for the Montagues.'

'I can explain everything,' said the Friar. 'It is all a mistake, a terrible mistake. They loved each other. The Nurse and I helped them to get married secretly. Now they are dead.'

Finally the Prince spoke.

'My friends Mercutio and Paris are dead. Tybalt is dead. Romeo and Juliet are dead. This is a terrible day for Verona. Lord Montague and Lord Capulet, shake hands. Your families must be friends. Love will change the world!'

1. **Watchman** : a kind of policeman.
2. **nuns** : religious women who live without men.
3. **stabbed** : killed with a knife.

Comprehension and Opinion

1 What happened in Part Six?

a. What did Romeo decide to do?
b. Why did Paris and Romeo fight?
c. Was Juliet really dead when Romeo saw her?
d. Why did Friar Laurence's plan not succeed?
e. How did Juliet kill herself?
f. What did the Prince say?

What do you think?

Who is responsible for the deaths? Will the Montagues and the Capulets be friends?

Past Simple Passive（過去時被動式）

2 We can write: *Romeo killed Paris.* **(Past Simple Active)**
or *Paris was killed by Romeo.* **(Past Simple Passive)**
Change these sentences in the same way from Active to Passive. Use *was* or *were* + the past participle.

a. Tybalt killed Mercutio and then Romeo killed Tybalt.

....

b. The Prince banished Romeo.

....

c. The Friar hid Romeo in his cell. Luckily, the Prince did not find him.

....

d. Juliet sent the Nurse to find Romeo. She took him to the garden of the Capulets at night.

....

e. The Capulets put Juliet's body in the tomb.

....

f. The soldiers prevented Friar John from reaching Mantua.

....

g. The Watchman found three dead bodies.

....

h. The Friar helped Romeo and Juliet.

....

i. Shakespeare wrote *Romeo and Juliet* and the actors* performed it in London. (*'by the actors' is not important, so forget it.)

....

The Verona Times

PET **3** **Read the newspaper article below and choose the correct word for each space. For each question, mark the letter next to the correct word – A, B, C or D.**

TRAGIC DEATH OF YOUNG LOVERS

In the middle (0) ...A..... the night, three deaths occurred at the Tomb of the Capulets. The Watchman discovered the body of Count Paris outside (1) .... Capulets' tomb. There was an even (2) .... sight inside. Juliet of the Capulets and Romeo of the Montagues (3) .... dead. (4) .... understood what had happened until Friar Laurence (5) .... his story. We now know that the teenagers were in love but had (6) .... the truth (7) .... their families had been enemies for centuries. They had got married (8) .... each other secretly. But when her parents ordered her to marry Paris, Juliet didn't know (9) .... to do. Read more about this tragedy in (10) .... newspaper.

	A	B	C	D
0.	(A) of	B at	C in	D by
1.	A of	B the	C a	D from
2.	A worst	B baddest	C worser	D worse
3.	A laid	B lying	C lay	D lied
4.	A Everybody	B All	C Nobody	D None
5.	A said	B discussed	C telled	D told
6.	A hided	B hidden	C hid	D hiding
7.	A although	B because	C when	D after
8.	A for	B with	C by	D to
9.	A how	B which	C what	D why
10.	A tomorrow's	B next	C following	D later

Lines from Shakespeare

4 **You will hear some famous lines from Shakespeare's original play. Remember that Shakespeare wrote 400 years ago, so the language is old-fashioned and difficult! Which character is speaking? Can you decide at which moment in the story?**

a. .... : Thou * wast the prettiest babe that e'r I nursed.
An I might live to see thee * married once, I have my wish.
* ***Thou, thee, thy****: old forms of 'you, you and your'.*

b. .... : For you and I are past our dancing days.

c. .... : It seems she hangs upon the cheek * of night
As a rich jewel in an Ethiope's ear.
* ***cheek****: the side of the face.*

d. .... : My only love sprung* from my only hate!
* ***sprung****: (past participle of 'to spring') come from.*

e. .... : But soft, what light through yonder * window breaks?
It is the east, and Juliet is the sun.
* ***yonder****: that.*

f. .... : See how she leans her cheek upon her hand.
O, that I were a glove upon that hand,
That I might touch that cheek!

g. .... : O Romeo, Romeo, wherefore art thou * Romeo?
Deny thy father and refuse thy name,
* ***Wherefore art thou****: Why are you called...*

h. .... : What's in a name? That which we call a rose
By any other word would smell as sweet.

i. .... : O, swear * not by the moon, th'inconstant moon *
* ***swear****: promise seriously.*
* ***th'inconstant moon****: the changeable moon.*

j. .... : Good night, good night. Parting is such sweet sorrow
That I shall say good night till it be morrow.

k. .... : Young men's love then lies
Not truly in their hearts, but in their eyes.

l. .... : A plague o' both your houses.*
They have made worms' meat of me.
* ***houses****: here, families.*

m. .... : For never was a story of more woe *
Than this of Juliet and her Romeo.
* ***woe****: sadness.*

Characters in the Play

5 Here are some opinions about the story. In each box, write: A if you agree. D if you disagree. ? if you are not sure.

	A	D	?
a. Romeo and Juliet were too young to love.	☐	☐	☐
b. Lord Capulet was a bad father.	☐	☐	☐
c. The Prince was not strict (= strong) enough.	☐	☐	☐
d. Lord Montague and Capulet were responsible for the lovers' deaths.	☐	☐	☐
e. Romeo was a murderer.	☐	☐	☐
f. Juliet was right to kill herself.	☐	☐	☐
g. Friar Laurence made a lot of mistakes.	☐	☐	☐
h. Tybalt was the cause of all the problems.	☐	☐	☐
i. Benvolio was the best person in the story.	☐	☐	☐
j. The Nurse was a foolish old woman.	☐	☐	☐

Compare your answers with your friend's.

All the Romeos and all the Juliets

6 Here is a short poem:

The Capulets hated the Montagues
who hated the Capulets;
there were angry words in Verona
and blood running in the streets.
But after the death of a boy and girl,
their love lived on to change the world,
and so does the love of all the Romeos and all the Juliets.

Today, there are modern Romeos and Juliets.

Maybe they come: from different social classes
or from opposite sides in a war
or from different races
or from different gangs
or from the supporters of different football teams
or from different galaxies!

Think of ideas for a story about one of these.

Maybe your 'Romeo and Juliet' will be as famous as Shakespeare's.

Juliet through the Centuries

Juliet Capulet is undoubtedly one of the best known characters of literature. She lived long ago, and yet people all over the world know her tragic love story. She and Romeo are considered the eternal [1] symbol of love, everywhere. There have been countless love stories, happy ones and sad ones. And yet, this tragic love story has been remembered and retold through the centuries, in many different ways.

Poets have written poems about the two young lovers. The great Italian poet, Dante Alighieri, mentions the two feuding families in his *Divina Commedia* (*Purgatorio*). Artists have created paintings on this subject. Musicians have written music for operas, symphonies and ballets, all based on Shakespeare's play. These are a few examples:

Vincenzo Bellini	*Capuleti e Montecchi*	(opera)	1830
Hector Berlioz	*Giulietta e Romeo*	(symphony)	1839
Charles Gounod	*Romeo and Juliet*	(opera)	1867
Peter I. Tchaikovsky	*Romeo and Juliet*	(tone poem)	1892
Sergei Prokofiev	*Romeo and Juliet*	(ballet)	1936

Gazing through a fish tank, the photogenic Leonardo DiCaprio captures the hearts of millions of teenage fans. A scene from Baz Luhrmann's *William Shakespeare's Romeo and Juliet* (1996).

1. **eternal** : lasting forever.

There have been numerous film productions, too. In 1968, Franco Zeffirelli directed the excellent film, *Romeo e Giulietta*. Another very recent film version is *Romeo and Juliet*, with Leonard DiCaprio.

The famous American musical *West Side Story* is a modern version of the eternal love story. West Side Story takes place in the immigrant neighbourhoods of New York City in the 1950s. Instead of two enemy families, there are two young enemy gangs. The famous American orchestra conductor and composer, Leonard Bernstein, wrote the exciting music for this wonderful musical.

A scene from the famous American musical *West Side Story* (1961) by Leonard Bernstein.

Juliet has been represented and interpreted in many different ways through the years. The Juliet we see in *West Side Story*, for example, represents the typical young girl of the twentieth century. She is very different from Shakespeare's heroine. [1] Her appearance, her language, her aspirations [2] and her life are very different. But the sentiments of love and passion remain the same through the centuries.

1. **heroine** : main female character in a play.
2. **aspirations** : strong desires.

PET

1 Look at the statements below and decide if each statement is correct or incorrect. If it is correct, mark A. If it is incorrect, mark B.

	A	B
1. Juliet and Romeo are considered the eternal symbol of love, all over the world.	☐	☐
2. Dante Alighieri mentions the two lovers in his *Divina Commedia.*	☐	☐
3. The Italian composer, Vincenzo Bellini, wrote a song about Juliet.	☐	☐
4. The Russian composer Prokofiev wrote a ballet called *Romeo and Juliet.*	☐	☐
5. Leonard Bernstein, the contemporary American composer, wrote a tone poem called *West Side Story.*	☐	☐
6. *West Side Story* takes place in New York City in the 1950s.	☐	☐
7. Instead of two feuding families, there are two enemy gangs.	☐	☐

INTERNET PROJECT

Choose one of the film productions mentioned above – Zeffirelli's *Romeo e Giulietta*, *Romeo and Juliet* with Leonardo DiCaprio, or *West Side Story* and use the internet to find out as much information about the film as possible.

Try and include the following:

- Director
- main actors with some biographical [1] information
- date of release [2]
- whether faithful [3] to the original
- setting
- critical acclaim [4]

1. **biographical** : describing a person's life.
2. **release** : when something is shown in public.
3. **faithful** : not changing any of the facts.
4. **acclaim** : public praise.

ROMEO AND JULIET

Playscript

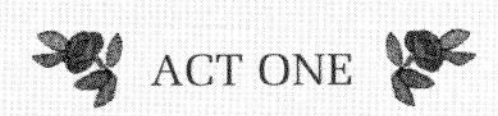

ACT ONE

THE MONTAGUES AND THE CAPULETS

In the beautiful city of Verona, there are two families – the Montagues and the Capulets. They hate each other. They have hated each other for hundreds of years. One day, the servants begin to fight in the streets.

SERVANTS OF THE MONTAGUES : The Montagues are better than the Capulets!

SERVANTS OF THE CAPULETS : Our masters, the Capulets, are better!

Then Benvolio and Tybalt arrive.

BENVOLIO : Stop fighting!

TYBALT : Fight with me, Benvolio.

BENVOLIO : No! Fighting is stupid!

TYBALT : Your sword is out. Fight!

Then Lord and Lady Capulet arrive. Lord Capulet is old but he wants to fight too.

LORD CAPULET : Bring me my sword.

LADY CAPULET : You are too old to fight. You don't need a sword, you need a crutch.

Then Lord and Lady Montague arrive. Soon everyone is fighting. It is very dangerous. At last, the Prince arrives. He is very angry.

PRINCE : Stop fighting! I want peace in my city.
Lord Capulet and Lord Montague, you are old but you are not wise. If your two families fight again, you will both die!

LORD CAPULET : I, Lord Capulet, promise not to fight again.

LORD MONTAGUE : I, Lord Montague, promise not to fight again.

The Prince is happy. Everyone goes away.

PAUSE

Lady Montague and Benvolio are talking.

BENVOLIO : Tybalt wants to kill all the Montagues. He is very dangerous.

LADY MONTAGUE : Where is my son, Romeo? Is he safe?

BENVOLIO : He is not here. He is walking by himself in the forest. He is sad.

LADY MONTAGUE : Why is he sad?

BENVOLIO : I don't know. But look, he is coming now. I will ask him.
Why are you unhappy, Romeo?

ROMEO : I am in love.

BENVOLIO : Who do you love?

ROMEO : I love sweet Rosaline. She is beautiful, intelligent and good. But she does not love me. That is why I am sad.

BENVOLIO : Forget her. There are many other girls.

ROMEO : No, I can never forget her.

PAUSE

Lord Capulet is talking to his wife, Lady Capulet.

LORD CAPULET : I am going to have a party. I will invite all the important people from Verona. But not the Montagues.

LADY CAPULET : You must invite Paris.

LORD CAPULET : Yes, I want him to meet Juliet. One day, they will get married.

LADY CAPULET : I like that idea. I will go and tell Juliet.

LORD CAPULET : Tell my servant to come here.

SERVANT : Yes, my Lord?

LORD CAPULET : Here is a list of guests. Go and invite them.

The servant meets Romeo and Benvolio in the street. He does not know that they are Montagues.

SERVANT : Can you help me? I can't read the names on this piece of paper.

BENVOLIO : Look, Romeo. Rosaline will be at the party.

ROMEO : I have an idea.

PAUSE

Lady Capulet is talking to Juliet. Juliet is thirteen years old. She has an old nurse who looks after her.

LADY CAPULET : You will meet Paris at the party. Perhaps you will marry him one day.

JULIET : Mother, I am too young to get married.

NURSE : I would love to see my little Juliet married. You will have happy days and happy nights.

SERVANT : The party is ready, my lady.

ACT TWO

THE GARDEN OF THE CAPULETS

Romeo is going to the party with Benvolio and his friend, Mercutio. They are all wearing masks. It is very dangerous for the Montagues and their friends to go to a party in the house of the Capulets.

ROMEO : Put on your masks. They must not recognise us. I cannot wait to see fair Rosaline.

SERVANT : Welcome, gentlemen. Come in. Dance and drink and eat. Enjoy yourselves.

As they go into the house, Romeo sees Juliet for the first time.
He forgets Rosaline! He falls in love! But Tybalt recognises Romeo's voice.

ROMEO : Who is that lady? She is more beautiful than the moon. I have never loved until now.

TYBALT : I know his voice. It is a Montague. I will kill him.

LORD CAPULET : Be calm, Tybalt. This is a party. I want no trouble.

Romeo goes to Juliet and talks to her. He does not know who she is.

ROMEO : My lips are ready to kiss you.

JULIET : But I do not know you.

ROMEO : I must kiss you.

JULIET : Here I am. My lips are here.

Romeo kisses Juliet. He kisses her a second time.

NURSE : Juliet, your mother wants you. You must come with me.

ROMEO : Excuse me, who is that girl?

NURSE : Young man, that is Juliet. She is a Capulet.

ROMEO : *(thinking aloud)* What! I am in love with the daughter of the enemy of my family.

JULIET : Nurse, who is that young man?

NURSE : That is Romeo. He is a Montague.

JULIET : Oh no! I am in love with the son of the enemy of my family. We can never get married.

After they leave the party, Mercutio and Benvolio look for Romeo.

MERCUTIO : Look! He is there in the shadows. What is he doing?

BENVOLIO : He is jumping the wall. He is going into the garden of the Capulets.

MERCUTIO : Romeo! Madman! Lover! He is going to look for Rosaline.

BENVOLIO : Quiet! You will make him angry. His love is blind.

MERCUTIO : Good night, Romeo. He is probably sitting under a tree, dreaming about that girl. He is mad.

Mercutio and Benvolio go home. The night is silent.

In the dark garden, Romeo suddenly sees a light. Juliet is standing on her balcony. She begins to speak to the night. She does not know that Romeo is listening.

JULIET : O Romeo, Romeo! Why is your name Romeo? Let's change our names. Then we can love. Forget that you are a Montague. Or, if you love me, I will not be a Capulet. Montague and Capulet are only names. A rose can have any name. It always smells sweet.

ROMEO : I will change my name for you.

JULIET : Who's there? Who is listening in the middle of the night?

ROMEO : It's me. Romeo.

JULIET : Why are you there?

ROMEO : I love you. And I know that you love me.

JULIET : What shall we do? Our families are enemies.

ROMEO : We must get married secretly. We will do it tomorrow. I will tell the Nurse where you must meet me. Will you marry me?

JULIET : Yes, Romeo. But will you be true?

ROMEO : Yes, my darling.

NURSE : Juliet! Juliet!

JULIET : Good night, Romeo. I must go. The Nurse is calling.

ROMEO : Good night, Juliet.

NURSE : Juliet! Juliet!

JULIET : I'm coming, Nurse. Good night.

ROMEO : Good night.

JULIET : Good night.

ROMEO : *(further away)* Good night.

JULIET : It is very sad and very sweet to say good night. But tomorrow, we will be married.

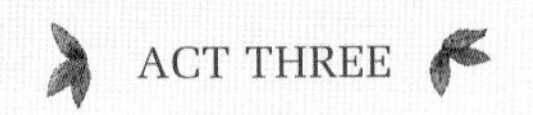

THE PRINCE OF CATS

Romeo goes to see Friar Laurence, his friend and teacher. The Friar is working in his garden. The sun is rising. It is a beautiful morning.

ROMEO : I want to get married.

FRIAR : To Rosaline?

ROMEO : No, to Juliet. I love her.

FRIAR : Good. Perhaps your marriage will make the Capulets and the Montagues friends. It is a good thing for Verona. I will help you.

Benvolio and Mercutio are looking for Romeo in the streets of Verona.

BENVOLIO : Poor Romeo. His heart is broken. Rosaline does not love him.

MERCUTIO : That's not his only problem. Tybalt has sent a letter to his house. He wants to fight him.

BENVOLIO : Tybalt is dangerous.

MERCUTIO : Yes. Tybalt is the Prince of Cats. He is an artist with his sword. Romeo is a lamb. He will die.

BENVOLIO : Quiet! Here comes Romeo.

ROMEO : Hello, Benvolio. Hello, Mercutio, my friend.

MERCUTIO : Are you still sad? Have you been crying all night for Rosaline? But look, here comes a fat old woman.

NURSE : Romeo, Romeo. I must talk with you, privately. Do you have any news for Juliet?

ROMEO : Yes. Tell Juliet to come to Friar Laurence's cell this afternoon. We will get married there.

NURSE : I love Juliet, sir. I remember when she was a little child. Look after her when you are her husband.

The Nurse goes back to Juliet. She tells her the news. The two lovers get ready for their secret wedding. In the afternoon, the sun is shining. Romeo goes secretly to Friar Laurence's cell.

FRIAR : The day is bright. It is a sign that the future will be happy.

ROMEO : I do not care if I die tomorrow. It is enough that Juliet is mine.

FRIAR : Don't be so passionate. It is better to love moderately. Then love will last longer.

At last Juliet arrives. She is very nervous. So is Romeo. They are very young but very much in love. Friar Laurence is like a father to them. He takes them into his cell and they are married.

But in the streets of Verona, there are problems.

TYBALT : Mercutio, where is Romeo?

MERCUTIO : I don't know. Why?

TYBALT : I want to kill him. He came to the party of the Capulets. You are his friend. You came with him. I want to fight you too.

MERCUTIO : Here is Romeo.

TYBALT : Fight, you villain!

ROMEO : I cannot fight you.

MERCUTIO : Romeo! Are you a coward? Tybalt!

TYBALT : What do you want?

MERCUTIO : I want one of your nine lives, Prince of Cats!

TYBALT : I will fight you as Romeo is too afraid to fight.

ROMEO : Stop fighting. The Prince will be angry. He will punish you. Stop, Tybalt. Stop, good Mercutio!

MERCUTIO : Aaaaagh! I am hurt. I am dying. Romeo, this quarrel between your families has killed me.

Mercutio falls to the ground and dies. It is Romeo's fault. His friend is dead.

ACT FOUR

FORTUNE'S FOOL

Romeo is angry. He loses control. He takes out his sword and fights with Tybalt. He kills him.

ROMEO : He killed my friend. Now he is dead. He is with Mercutio.

BENVOLIO : Romeo, you must escape. The people are coming. The Prince will punish you with death...

ROMEO : Oh, I am Fortune's fool! I must go.

PRINCE : What is happening? How did Tybalt die?

BENVOLIO : Romeo wanted to stop the fight. But Tybalt killed Mercutio. Then Romeo killed Tybalt.

PRINCE : Romeo must leave Verona. He has murdered Tybalt. If I find him in Verona, he will die.

LADY CAPULET : Tybalt is dead. The Montagues must pay for this. Benvolio is lying. Romeo is a murderer and must die.

Juliet is waiting for Romeo, her new husband. She wants the night to come so that they can be together. But when the Nurse arrives, she brings bad news.

NURSE : He is dead!

JULIET : What? Is Romeo dead?

NURSE : No, Tybalt is dead. Romeo has killed him. He must leave Verona.

JULIET : Did Romeo kill my cousin? He is a villain. But I love him.

NURSE : Your father and mother are crying for Tybalt.

JULIET : I will cry for him too. But I will cry longer for Romeo. I will never see him again. I will kill myself.

NURSE : No. Romeo is hiding with Friar Laurence. I will bring him to you.

The Nurse comes to find Romeo. He is talking to Friar Laurence.

ROMEO : Everything is finished. I will kill myself with this knife.

FRIAR : No, be brave. You must go to Mantua. You will be safe there. I will send you news about Juliet. One day, you will be together again. But tonight, go with the Nurse. See Juliet for the last time.

NURSE : Come with me. Here is the house of the Capulets. Here is a ladder. Climb up and go through the window.

So Romeo spends his marriage night with Juliet.

Downstairs, in the house of the Capulets, Lord and Lady Capulet are talking. Lord Paris is with them.

LORD CAPULET : I will talk to Juliet. She will marry you next Thursday. Tybalt is dead. There must be something good for the Capulet family – Juliet's wedding! I am her father. She will do as I say. Wife, see Juliet in the morning and tell her. She will marry Paris.

In the morning, Romeo leaves Juliet. He must escape to Mantua before the Prince finds him.

JULIET : Must you go? It is still night. The nightingale is singing, not the lark.

ROMEO : Look at the sky. The sun is rising. But I want to stay.

JULIET : Go. It is dangerous for you here. But I want you to stay. Goodbye, sweet Romeo. Will I ever see you again?

ROMEO : Goodbye. I will think of you every second of the day.

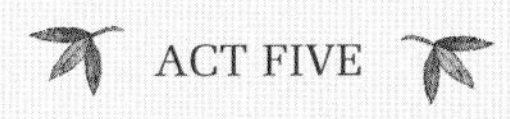

MY LADY'S DEAD!

Lady Capulet tells Juliet that she must marry Paris.

LADY CAPULET : You will get married to Paris early next Thursday morning.

JULIET : No, Mother. As you know, I hate Romeo. He has killed my cousin. But I'd rather marry Romeo than Paris.

JULIET *(thinking)* : I am already married.

LORD CAPULET : Paris is a fine gentleman. Marry him on Thursday or never speak to me again.

NURSE : Please don't be angry with my little Juliet, sir.

LORD CAPULET : Shut up, you fat old fool. I have decided. If you don't obey me,

I will throw you out in the streets. Goodbye. Remember, on Thursday, you are going to be married.

LADY CAPULET : Goodbye, daughter. You must obey your father.

JULIET : Nurse, tell me, what should I do?

NURSE : Well, Romeo is not here. Paris is a fine gentleman, it's true. He is more handsome than Romeo. Forget Romeo and marry Paris.

JULIET : Do you speak from your heart? *(thinking)* I cannot trust her. I will ask the Friar for advice. He is the only person who can help me.

The Friar is very worried. He is talking to Paris.

PARIS : I am going to marry Juliet.

FRIAR : Does she love you?

PARIS : I don't know. We haven't talked about love because she is weeping for her cousin's death. But our marriage will make her happy again.

FRIAR : But look, here comes Juliet.

PARIS : Welcome, my lady and my wife. Have you come to tell the Friar that you love me?

JULIET : I cannot answer that. But please, let me talk to the Friar privately.

PARIS : Goodbye. I know that you love me. I will see you on Thursday in the church.

FRIAR : Be happy, Juliet. I have a plan. You and Romeo will be together.

JULIET : Tell me! What is it?

FRIAR : Go home and agree to marry Paris. On Wednesday night, go to your bedroom alone. Take this bottle and drink the liquid. It is a special potion. You will sleep for forty-two hours. Your family will think that you are dead. They will carry you to the tomb of the Capulets. Meanwhile, I will send a message to Romeo. He will come secretly to the tomb. When you wake up, you can escape together. Are you brave enough to do this, Juliet?

JULIET : Give me the bottle, Friar. Love will give me strength.

Juliet goes home.

JULIET : Mother, Father, I have changed my mind. I will obey you. I have seen Lord Paris at the Friar's cell and I've told him that I love him.

LORD CAPULET : Good, you are a good daughter.

LADY CAPULET : You have made your old father happy.

JULIET : Now I am going to my room to pray. Do not come with me, Nurse, I want to be alone.

PAUSE

JULIET : Here is the bottle. I am afraid. Perhaps it is poison. Or perhaps I will wake in the tomb and Romeo will not be there. I will be alone in the middle of all the dead bodies with my dead cousin, Tybalt. It will be terrible.

Bravely, Juliet picks up the bottle and raises it to her lips.

JULIET : Romeo, Romeo, I drink to you!

She drinks. She falls on the bed and sleeps...

The next morning, it is Thursday. The Nurse comes to wake her up for her marriage.

NURSE : You lazy girl. Why are you still sleeping? You mustn't lie in bed on your wedding day... . Help! Help! My lady's dead! My lady's dead!

Lord and Lady Capulet take Juliet to the tomb of the Capulets. They are very sad. Their only child is dead.

FRIAR : I have sent Friar John to Mantua to tell Romeo to come back to Verona. He will be here when Juliet wakes up.

NURSE : Oh sad day! Oh unhappy day! Oh terrible day!

ACT SIX

WITH A KISS, I DIE

Romeo is in Mantua. His servant, Balthasar, comes to bring him the latest news.

ROMEO : I have been dreaming about Juliet. Even a dream of love is sweet.

BALTHASAR : Juliet is dead.

ROMEO : What! I will ride to Verona tonight. I will kiss her for the last time. Then I will drink poison. If Juliet is dead, I will die too.

In the middle of the night, Romeo arrives at the tomb of the Capulets. Paris is also there with his servant.

PARIS : I have come to put flowers on Juliet's grave. But who is this? You are a Montague, the one who killed Tybalt. You must die.

ROMEO : I do not know you. Go away if you want to live. Do not fight with me. I am desperate. I am stronger than tigers or the roaring sea.

PARIS : I arrest you, murderer.

They fight.

ROMEO : It is Paris! I have killed him. Balthasar told me that he wanted to marry Juliet. We are both unlucky. But where is Juliet? I must look at her beauty for the last time.

PAUSE

ROMEO : Oh my love, my wife! Death has kissed you. But you are still beautiful. Death is jealous. He keeps you here as his lover. I will also stay here. But let me kiss you. With a kiss, I die.

Romeo kisses Juliet. He takes a cup of poison out of his pocket and raises it to his lips.

FRIAR : Romeo! Romeo!

Friar John has come to Friar Laurence's cell.

FRIAR : Have you given my letter to Romeo, Friar John?

JOHN : No, Friar Laurence. I did not reach Mantua. There was plague in one of the villages on the road and the soldiers did not let me pass.

FRIAR : What! This is bad news. If Juliet wakes when Romeo is not there, she will be afraid. I must go to her.

PAUSE

FRIAR : I can see a light in the tomb. Who is looking among the skulls and the worms?

BALTHASAR : It is my master, Romeo.

FRIAR : I must go to him. Romeo! Romeo!

But when the Friar goes inside the tomb, Romeo has already drunk the poison. He is dead.

Juliet wakes up and sees the Friar.

JULIET : Where is Romeo?

FRIAR : He is dead. But we must go. The watchman is coming. Come with me.

JULIET : No, I will stay with Romeo. I will drink poison too – but the cup is empty. Let me kiss his lips. They are still warm. I can hear people coming. Quick, here is Romeo's dagger. Let me die!

Everyone arrives at the tomb of the Capulets. It is too late. Romeo and Juliet have both died. Their great love story is finished.

WATCHMAN : Here is the body of Paris. And here are the bodies of a boy and girl...

LORD CAPULET : Juliet! There is blood and a dagger. Our only daughter is dead. This is a terrible day for the Capulets.

LORD MONTAGUE : Last night, my wife died from a broken heart because Romeo was banished from Verona. Now he is dead, poisoned. This is a terrible day for the Montagues.

FRIAR : I can explain everything. It is all a mistake, a terrible mistake. They loved each other. The Nurse and I helped them to get married secretly. Now they are dead.

PRINCE : My friends Mercutio and Paris are dead. Tybalt is dead. Romeo and Juliet are dead. This is a terrible day for Verona. Lord Montague and Lord Capulet, shake hands. Your families must be friends. Love will change the world.

EXIT TEST

PET **1** **Read the text below and choose the correct word for each space.**
For each question, mark the letter next to the correct word – A, B, C or D.

(0) ...A... love bring happiness? Romeo and Juliet (1) .... in love as soon as they saw each other. In other (2) ...., it was love at first (3) .... Usually, falling in love is a very happy experience that (4) .... lead to marriage and a lifetime together. (5) ...., in this case, the love of the teenage couple caused a series of problems. Mercutio, Tybalt and Paris all (6) .... In addition Romeo and Juliet killed (7) .... as a result of a terrible misunderstanding. (8) .... was responsible? Was it Friar Laurence or their parents or Tybalt? What (9) .... you (10) .... ?

0.	**(A)** Does	**B** Do	**C** Why	**D** Is
1.	**A** fell	**B** falled	**C** felt	**D** feeled
2.	**A** terms	**B** words	**C** wise	**D** example
3.	**A** seeing	**B** look	**C** sight	**D** glance
4.	**A** maybe	**B** may	**C** must	**D** does
5.	**A** Although	**B** And	**C** However	**D** Also
6.	**A** dead	**B** death	**C** dyed	**D** died
7.	**A** themself	**B** theirselves	**C** herself	**D** themselves
8.	**A** What	**B** How	**C** Which	**D** Who
9.	**A** do	**B** are	**C** does	**D** have
10.	**A** thinking	**B** thought	**C** think	**D** agree

PET **2** **These questions are about the whole story.**
For each question, mark the letter next to the best answer – A, B, C or D.

1. Which of these is most probably one of the main reasons why Shakespeare chose to write about the story of *Romeo and Juliet*?

A ☐ Because it was a story about Renaissance Italy.
B ☐ Because it was a story about love and death.
C ☐ Because it was a story about secrets and lies.
D ☐ Because it was a story about people from his own time.

2. What do we learn about Romeo from the play?

A ☐ He was clever and thoughtful.
B ☐ Juliet was the only girl he ever loved.
C ☐ He sometimes acted too quickly without thinking.
D ☐ He defended his own family passionately.

3. Friar Laurence

A ☐ tried to help Romeo and Juliet but failed.
B ☐ gave poison to Juliet.
C ☐ acted kindly and openly.
D ☐ lived in a prison cell.

4. The Prince banished Romeo

A ☐ because it is wrong to kill.
B ☐ because he married Juliet without permission.
C ☐ because he was a Montague.
D ☐ because the Capulets wanted revenge.

5. Which of the following is the best overall description of the story of *Romeo and Juliet*?

A ☐ Two teenage lovers overcome their problems despite the disapproval of their parents.
B ☐ Two teenage lovers die as a result of a secret plan that went wrong.
C ☐ The love between two teenagers ends in death because of the feud between their families.
D ☐ Two families end their long-standing quarrel as a result of a secret marriage between their children.

PET **3** **Look at the statements below about Shakespeare and *Romeo and Juliet*. Read the appropriate parts of the story to decide if each statement is correct or incorrect. If it is correct, mark A. If it is not correct, mark B.**

		A	B
1.	Juliet was a Capulet and Romeo was a Montague.	☐	☐
2.	First of all, Juliet's parents wanted her to marry Tybalt.	☐	☐
3.	Juliet's father encouraged Tybalt to fight Romeo.	☐	☐
4.	The Nurse discovered Juliet talking to Romeo from the balcony.	☐	☐
5.	Friar Laurence agreed to help them to bring peace to the families.	☐	☐
6.	Mercutio fought Tybalt after Romeo had refused the challenge.	☐	☐
7.	Romeo visited Juliet for the last time with the Nurse's help.	☐	☐
8.	The Nurse advised Juliet to forget Romeo and marry Paris.	☐	☐
9.	Paris wanted to fight Romeo because Romeo had married Juliet secretly.	☐	☐
10.	When the Friar arrived at the tomb, both Romeo and Juliet were dead.	☐	☐

Answer to question 9, page 43.
There are 59 people in the room. Did you include the reporter?

Focus on the context

4 **Answer the following questions.**

a. Where and when was William Shakespeare born?
b. What do you remember of his life?
c. What do you remember of the period he lived in?
d. What do you know about life in Verona during the Renaissance?

Focus on the story

5 **Answer the following questions.**

a. For how long had the Montagues and the Capulets hated each other?
b. Who did Romeo love at the beginning of the story?
c. Who did Lord Capulet hope Juliet would marry?
d. Where did Romeo meet Juliet for the first time?
e. Where did Romeo and Juliet get married?
f. What was Tybalt's nickname?
g. Who killed Mercutio?
h. Why did Romeo kill Tybalt?
i. What did the Prince of Verona decide to do when he discovered that Romeo had killed Tybalt?
j. Which city did Friar Lawrence tell Romeo to go to?
k. What was Friar Lawrence's plan to stop Juliet from marrying Paris?
l. Did the plan work?
m. What happened when Juliet woke up?
n. What did the Prince of Verona tell Lord Montague and Lord Capulet to do at the end?

6 Complete this crossword.

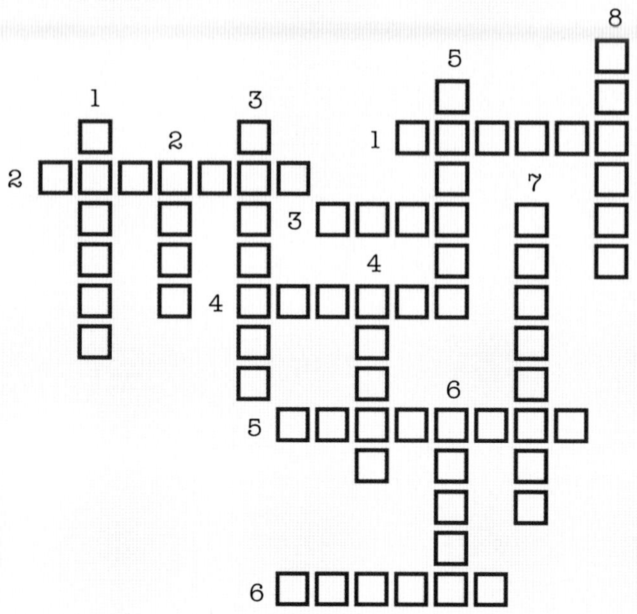

ACROSS:

1. Friar Laurence gave Juliet a mysterious .... to drink the night before her wedding to Paris.
2. A famous scene in the play shows Juliet on her .... .
3. Romeo's last words were: 'With a ...., I die.'
4. Tybalt was Juliet's .... .
5. .... was Romeo's friend.
6. Juliet stabbed herself with this.

DOWN:

1. Romeo climbed up a .... to reach Juliet's room.
2. Romeo and Juliet got married in this.
3. A 'Fortune's Fool' is an .... person.
4.
5. Romeo killed himself with this.
6. Lord Capulet was Tybalt's .... .
7. The Montagues and Capulets were always .... in the streets.
8. The Prince of Verona decided to .... Romeo from the city.

Romeo and Juliet

KEY TO THE ACTIVITIES AND EXIT TEST

KEY TO THE ACTIVITIES

Page 15 – exercise 1
1. 1564 **2.** third **3.** glove-maker
4. three **5.** Only a little **6.** deer
7. London **8.** writer **9.** copying
10. poems **11.** his birthday
12. Stratford

Page 15 – exercise 2
1. B **2.** A **3.** B **4.** B **5.** B **6.** A **7.** B
8. A **9.** A **10.** B

Page 15 – exercise 3
1. It was written in the middle of the 1590s.
3. Chaucer respected Dante as the greatest European poet.
4. Many, not all, of Shakespeare's plays are located in Italy.
5. In England the legend of Romeo and Juliet had been very popular for a long time.
7. In his play Juliet is only thirteen years old.
10. It ends in death.

PART ONE

Page 25 – exercise 1
a. The Montagues and the Capulets.
b. No.
c. Because they were fighting in the streets.
d. Because Rosaline did not love him.
e. The servant asked them to read the list of names of people to invite.
f. They wanted her to marry him.

Page 25 – exercise 2a
a. beautiful
b. dangerous
c. old
d. angry
e. old / wise
f. sad / long
g. terrible
h. heavy / light / serious / foolish
i. beautiful / intelligent / good
j. happy / happy

Page 26 – exercise 2b
Open answer.

Page 26 – exercise 2c
1. cruel / kind **2.** fat / thin
3. friendly / unfriendly **4.** hard-working / lazy **5.** happy / sad
6. intelligent / stupid **7.** modest / proud **8.** poor / rich **9.** short / tall
10. terrible / wonderful

Page 27 – exercise 2d
happy: ecstatic, glad, joyful

sad: depressed, miserable, unhappy
rich: affluent, prosperous, wealthy
beautiful: attractive, handsome, pretty
wonderful: excellent, fantastic, great
thin: slim, skinny, slender

Page 28 – exercise 3
Open answers.

Page 29 – exercise 4
a. son **b.** aunt **c.** daughter
d. father **e.** cousin **f.** mother
g. brothers **h.** sisters **i.** parents
j. wife **k.** husband **l.** uncle
m. grandmother **n.** nephew

The words reading down are:
STAR-CROSSED LOVERS

Page 30 – exercise 5
1. B **2.** B **3.** B **4.** B **5.** A **6.** A

Tapescript

The Queen of the Fairies

Romeo is with his friend Mercutio. They are talking:

***Mercutio**:* *What's the matter, Romeo? Why are you so quiet tonight?*

***Romeo**:* *I am unhappy. I am in love.*

***Mercutio**:* *Don't be stupid. We'll be late for the party. There will be lots of beautiful girls there.*

***Romeo**:* *I am very tired. Last night, I dreamt about sweet Rosaline. I didn't sleep well.*

***Mercutio**:* *Ah! The Queen of the Fairies has been with you. Her name is Queen Mab. She is very small. She rides over our noses while we are sleeping. She gives us our dreams. When she visits them, girls dream about kisses. Soldiers dream about killing. Lovers dream about love. She is very dangerous. She can change our lives.*

Page 30 – exercise 6
1. Mercutio tells Romeo not to be stupid.
2. Romeo dreamt about Rosaline.
3. Queen Mab is a fairy.
4. She gives us our dreams.

Page 30 – exercise 7
Open answers.

Page 31 – exercise 8
Open answers.

Page 31 – exercise 9
Open answers.

PART TWO

Page 38 – exercise 1
a. Because it was dangerous for the Montagues to go to the house of the Capulets.
b. He fell in love.
c. They kissed each other.
d. He jumped over the wall.
e. She was on her balcony.
f. They decided to get married secretly.

Page 38 – exercise 2
a. immediately **b.** angrily **c.** kindly

d. violently **e.** loudly **f.** lovingly
g. stupidly **h.** passionately
i. beautifully **j.** anxiously

Page 39 – exercise 3

a. was trying / arrived **b.** saw / was fighting **c.** was walking / met
d. was helping / came **e.** were kissing / saw **f.** recognised / was talking
g. was standing / began **h.** was saying / called **i.** was using / phoned **j.** were watching / left **k.** did not want / was playing **l.** did not answer / was watching **m.** were fighting / arrived

Page 40 – exercise 4

1. ring **2.** wedding **3.** bride
4. bridegroom **5.** church **6.** priest
7. happy **8.** divorce **9.** secretly
10. heart **11.** love **12.** sight
13. girlfriend

Juliet's words are: PARTING IS SUCH SWEET SORROW

Page 41 – exercise 5

Open answers.

Page 41 – exercise 6

1. A **2.** C **3.** B **4.** B **5.** B **6.** C **7.** A
8. How many people are in the room?
9. 59

Tapescript

The Party

Here is a reporter describing the party at the house of the Capulets.
'I am standing in the big hall of the house of the Capulets. I am at the top of the stairs at the south entrance.
From here, I can see the whole room.
Lord Capulet and Tybalt are standing in the centre of the room. They are watching three mysterious strangers in masks who have just come through the door. Perhaps they are Montagues. Is that why they are wearing masks? Will there be another fight?
Lady Capulet is standing at the bottom of the stairs. Her young beautiful daughter, Juliet, is dancing with Paris. People say that they will get married one day. Juliet's Nurse is near the couple. She is standing between the stairs and the dinner table. She is looking at the food and wine.
There are thirty other guests in the room and thirteen servants. Also, there is a group of six musicians who are playing on a balcony above the dancers. It is a wonderful party. All the most important and famous people from Verona are here – except the Montagues!'
Here is the question:
How many people are in the room?

Page 43 – exercise 7

Open answer.

Page 44 – exercise 8

Open answer.

Page 44 – exercise 9

1. F **2.** B **3.** H **4.** D **5.** C

A Walk through Verona

Page 49 – exercise 1

1. C **2.** B **3.** A **4.** B **5.** C **6.** B

PART THREE

Page 56 – exercise 1

a. He wanted the Montagues and the Capulets to be friends.
b. Tybalt.

c. To tell Juliet to come to the Friar's cell.
d. Romeo and Juliet were married.
e. He had married Juliet, Tybalt's cousin.
f. Mercutio died.

Page 56 – exercise 2

a. lion **b.** pig **c.** horse **d.** mouse
e. donkey **f.** fox **g.** dog **h.** owl
i. pig **j.** swan

Page 57 – exercise 3

1. been sad since
2. has Juliet known
3. known Romeo for
4. have they fought
5. fought them for
6. lived here for
7. tended Juliet since
8. since she was

Page 58 – exercise 4

1. is my Nurse
2. is she late
3. you seen Romeo
4. news do you have
5. did Romeo say
6. did Romeo say
7. Romeo in love with me
8. he send a letter

Tapescript

The Nurse and Juliet

The Nurse has returned from the city where she has seen Romeo. Juliet wants to know the news but the Nurse makes her wait.
Listen carefully. Write down Juliet's questions.

Juliet: *Where is my Nurse? Why is she late? Ah, she's here. Have you seen Romeo?*

Nurse: *I am very tired. I have run from the town. My bones ache.*

Juliet: *What news do you have?*

Nurse: *Well, I have seen Romeo. He is handsome, young and polite. But have you had dinner yet?*

Juliet: *Nurse, don't ask stupid questions. What did Romeo say?*

Nurse: *My head aches. I am very tired.*

Juliet: *I am sorry for you. But sweet Nurse, what did Romeo say?*

Nurse: *He says... Where is your mother?*

Juliet: *She's in the house. But please be quick. Is Romeo in love with me?*

Nurse: *Don't be angry. I have run all over the city for you. Next time, go and ask Romeo yourself.*

Juliet: *Sweet Nurse, please tell me. Did he send a letter?*

Nurse: *He wants to marry you at Friar Laurence's cell this afternoon.*

Juliet: *Aaah! Thank you, Nurse.*

Page 59 – exercise 5

2. told **3.** decided **4.** went **5.** saw
6. kissed **7.** jumped **8.** talked
9. met **10.** got **11.** fought **12.** died
Open answers.

PART FOUR

Page 68 – exercise 1

a. Because Tybalt had killed Mercutio.
b. He decided to banish Romeo from Verona.
c. No, she still loved him.
d. To Mantua.
e. Because he was going to marry Juliet.
f. Because she loved Romeo and she saw only bad things in them.

Page 68 – exercise 2

a. unluckiest **b.** luck **c.** Luckily
d. luck **e.** lucky **f.** unlucky
g. luckier **h.** Unluckily **i.** luck
j. luckiest

Page 69 – exercise 3

Open answers.

Page 69 – exercise 4

a. already / still / yet
b. still / already / yet / still
c. already / still / yet / still
d. already / yet / still

Page 70 – exercise 5

1. B **2.** A **3.** B **4.** C **5.** A **6.** C

Tapescript

Four Zodiac Signs

Here are the horoscopes for next year.

First of all, here is the horoscope for Capricorn. Capricorns are born between the 22nd of December and the 20th of January.
Next year, Capricorns will be very successful in their jobs. They will fall in love. They will meet lots of people and have a good time. They will go to many interesting places all over the world. They will feel very healthy all year.
The horoscope is not so good for Cancer. Cancers have their birthday between June the 22nd and July the 23rd.
Cancers will have bad luck in their jobs. They will also have broken hearts. But they will meet many interesting people and go to lots of parties. They will travel to a few places. They will be ill in the second half of the year.
Leos are born between July the 24th and August 23rd. They will enjoy their work very much next year. Nothing special will happen in love or in their social life. But they will have lots of time for travelling and will visit many interesting places. They will feel very well all year.
Finally, Librans. Their birthdays are between September the 24th and October the 23rd. They must be very careful in their work. They may lose their jobs. If they have September birthdays, they will have broken hearts. But if they are born after the New Moon on the sixth of October, they will fall in love next year. Librans mustn't expect a good social life or a lot of travel next year. And it is a very bad year for their health!

Page 71 – exercise 6

Open answer.

Page 71 – exercise 7
Open answer.

Life in Renaissance Verona

Page 74 – exercise 1
1. C **2.** B **3.** D **4.** B **5.** A

Page 75 – exercise 2
a. silk **b.** jewel **c.** tailor **d.** dagger **e.** ball **f.** horse **g.** unisex

PART FIVE

Page 82 – exercise 1
a. She told her that she would marry Paris.
b. He said he would throw her out in the street.
c. She told her to forget Romeo and marry Paris.
d. For forty-two hours.
e. 'Romeo, Romeo, I drink to you.'
f. To tell Romeo the plan.

Page 82 – exercise 2
a. had been / saw **b.** had heard / knew **c.** challenged / had gone **d.** had killed / lost **e.** sent / had killed **f.** did not know / had married **g.** had helped / told **h.** drank / had given **i.** had drunk / fell **j.** had thought / thought

Page 83 – exercise 3
1. C **2.** B **3.** A **4.** C **5.** B

Page 85 – exercise 4
Open answers.

Page 85 – exercise 5
Open answers.

Page 86 – exercise 6
Open answer.

Page 86 – exercise 7
1. Benvolio wanted to make peace and Tybalt wanted to fight.
2. Romeo walked alone in the forest because he loved Rosaline.
3. The party was at the house of Lord and Lady Capulet.
4. Tybalt recognised him.
5. They kissed twice.
6. They talked at night.
7. TRUE.
8. No, he was a friend of Romeo's.
9. He called him the 'Prince of Cats'.
10. The Nurse thought Paris was more handsome than Romeo.
11. He will send Friar John.
12. She will sleep for forty-two hours after she has drunk the liquid.

Tapescript

True or False

Here are twelve statements about the story.

Number One:
Benvolio wanted to fight and Tybalt wanted to make peace.

Number Two:
Romeo walked alone in the forest because he loved Juliet.

Number Three:
The party was at the house of Lord and Lady Montague.

Number Four:
Nobody recognised Romeo at the party.

Number Five:
Romeo and Juliet kissed only once at the party.

Number Six:
Romeo talked to Juliet in the garden

the morning after the party.

Number Seven:

Friar Laurence was Romeo's teacher and friend.

Number Eight:

Mercutio was a member of the Montague family.

Number Nine:

Mercutio called Tybalt 'the Prince of Ghosts'.

Number Ten:

The Nurse thought that Romeo was more handsome than Paris.

Number Eleven:

Friar Laurence will send Friar Joe to Mantua.

Number Twelve:

Juliet will sleep for forty-two hours after she is taken to the tomb.

Page 87 – exercise 8

Open answers.

PART SIX

Page 94 – exercise 1

a. He decided to go to the tomb and kill himself.
b. They both loved Juliet.
c. No.
d. Because Friar John did not reach Mantua.
e. With Romeo's dagger.
f. 'Love will change the world!'

Page 94 – exercise 2

a. Mercutio was killed by Tybalt and then Tybalt was killed by Romeo.
b. Romeo was banished by the Prince.
c. Romeo was hidden by the Friar in his cell. Luckily, he wasn't found by the Prince.
d. The Nurse was sent by Juliet to find Romeo. He was taken to the garden of the Capulets at night by the Nurse.
e. Juliet's body was put in the tomb by the Capulets.
f. Friar John was prevented from reaching Mantua by the soldiers.
g. Three dead bodies were found by the Watchman.
h. Romeo and Juliet were helped by the Friar.
i. Romeo and Juliet was written by Shakespeare and it was performed in London.

Page 95 – exercise 3

1. B **2.** D **3.** C **4.** C **5.** D **6.** B **7.** B
8. D **9.** C **10.** A

Page 96 – exercise 4

a. The Nurse **b.** Lord Capulet
c. Romeo **d.** Juliet **e.** Romeo
f. Romeo. **g.**, **h.**, **i.**, **j.** Juliet **k.** Friar Laurence **l.** Mercutio **m.** The Prince.

Page 97 – exercise 5

Open answers.

Page 97 – exercise 6

Open answer.

Juliet through the centuries

Page 100 – exercise 1

1. A **2.** A **3.** B **4.** A **5.** B **6.** A **7.** A

Internet Project

Page 100

Very good websites for information on films are:
www.imdb.com
(the internet movie database)
www.allmovie.com

1 1.A, 2.B, 3.C, 4.B, 5.C, 6.D, 7.D, 8.D, 9.A, 10.C

2 1.B, 2.C, 3.A, 4. A, 5. C

3 1.A, 2.B, 3.B, 4.B, 5.A, 6.A, 7.A, 8.A, 9.B, 10.B

Focus on the context

4

a. In Stratford-upon-Avon on 23rd April, 1564.

b. *Possible answer:*
He was the third child of John Shakespeare and Mary Arden. He went to Stratford Grammar School but did not go to university. He married Anne Hathaway when he was eighteen and they had three children. He went to London and quickly became popular as a writer. He died in 1616 on his birthday and was buried in Stratford. He left his 'second-best bed' to his wife in his will.

c. *Possible answer:*
Elizabeth I was the Queen of England and during her reign, the country had made great progress in many areas and had become a major power in Europe.

d. Open answer.

Focus on the story

5

a. For hundreds of years.

b. Rosaline.

c. Paris.

d. At Lord Capulet's party.

e. In Friar Laurence's cell.

f. The Prince of Cats.

g. Tybalt.

h. Because he was angry that Tybalt had killed Mercutio and he lost control.

i. He decided to banish Romeo from Verona.

j. Mantua.

k. He told Juliet to drink a special potion the night before the wedding. It would make her sleep for forty-two hours and her family would think she was dead. Romeo would then return secretly and when Juliet woke up, they would escape together.

l. No, because Friar John did not reach Mantua to deliver Friar Laurence's message to Romeo. Balthasar, Romeo's servant, arrived to tell Romeo that Juliet was dead. Romeo returned to Verona. He saw Juliet and believed that she was dead, and took some poison to kill himself.

m. She saw that Romeo was dead, she took his dagger and killed herself.

n. To shake hands and become friends.

6

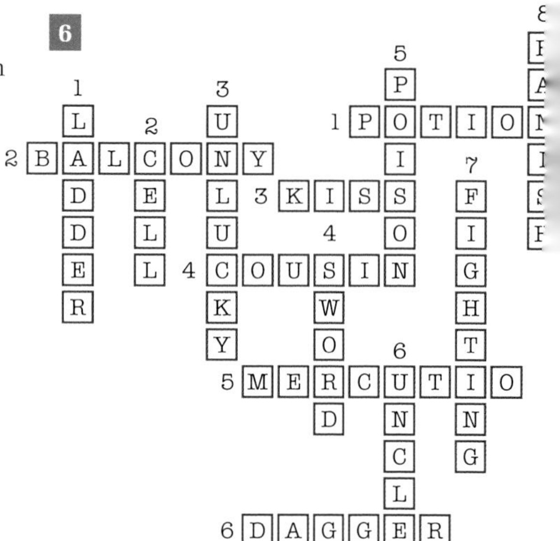

Black Cat English Readers

Level 1A
- Peter Pan CD-ROM
- Zorro!
- American Folk Tales
- The True Story of Pocahontas
- Davy Crockett

Level 1B
- Great Expectations
- Rip Van Winkle and The Legend of Sleepy Hollow
- The Happy Prince and The Selfish Giant CD-ROM
- The American West
- Halloween Horror

Level 1C
- The Adventures of Tom Sawyer CD-ROM
- The Adventures of Huckleberry Finn
- The Wonderful Wizard of Oz CD-ROM
- The Secret of the Stones
- The Wind in the Willows

Level 1D
- The Black Arrow
- Around the World in Eighty Days CD-ROM
- Little Women
- Beauty and the Beast
- Black Beauty

Level 2A
- Oliver Twist CD-ROM
- King Authur and his Knights
- Oscar Wilde's Short Stories
- Robin Hood
- British and American Festivities

Level 2B
- David Copperfield
- Animal Tales
- The Fisherman and his Soul
- The Call of the Wild
- Ghastly Ghosts!

Level 3 A
- Alice's Adventures in Wonderland
- The Jumping Frog
- Hamlet
- The Secret Garden CD-ROM
- Great English Monarchs and their Times

Level 3B
- True Adventure Stories

Level 4A
- The £1,000,000 Bank Note
- Jane Eyre
- Sherlock Holmes Investigates
- Gulliver's Travels
- The Strange Case of Dr Jekyll and Mr Hyde

Level 4B
- Romeo and Juliet CD-ROM
- Treasure Island
- The Phantom of the Opera
- Classic Detective Stories
- Alien at School

Level 5A
- A Christmas Carol
- The Tragedy of Dr Faustus
- Washington Square
- A Midsummer Night's Dream
- American Horror

Level 5B
- Much Ado about Nothing
- The Canterbury Tales
- Dracula
- The Last of the Mohican
- The Big Mistake and Other Stories

Level 5C
- The Age of Innocence

Level 6A
- Pride and Prejudice
- Robinson Crusoe
- A Tale of Two Cities
- Frankenstein
- The X-File: Squeeze

Level 6B
- Emma
- The Scarlet Letter
- Tess of the d'Urbervilles
- The Murders in the Rue Morgue and the Purloined Letter
- The Problem of Cell 13

BLACK CAT ENGLISH CLUB

Membership Application Form

BLACK CAT ENGLISH CLUB is for those who love English reading and seek for better English to share and learn with fun together.

Benefits offered:
- *Membership Card*
- *Member badge, poster, bookmark*
- *Book discount coupon*
- *Black Cat English Reward Scheme*
- *English learning e-forum*
- *Surprise gift and more...*

Simply fill out the application form below and fax it back to 2565 1113.

Join Now! It's FREE exclusively for readers who have purchased *Black Cat English Readers* **!**

The book(or book set) that you have purchased: ____________________

English Name: ______________ (Surname) ____________________ (Given Name)

Chinese Name: ____________________

Address: ____________________

Tel: ____________________ Fax: ____________________

Email: ____________________

(Login password for e-forum will be sent to this email address.)

Sex: ❑ Male ❑ Female

Education Background: ❑ Primary 1-3 ❑ Primary 4-6 ❑ Junior Secondary Education (F1-3) ❑ Senior Secondary Education (F4-5) ❑ Matriculation ❑ College ❑ University or above

Age: ❑ 6 - 9 ❑ 10 - 12 ❑ 13 - 15 ❑ 16 - 18 ❑ 19 - 24 ❑ 25 - 34 ❑ 35 - 44 ❑ 45 - 54 ❑ 55 or above

Occupation: ❑ Student ❑ Teacher ❑ White Collar ❑ Blue Collar ❑ Professional ❑ Manager ❑ Business Owner ❑ Housewife ❑ Others (please specify: ______________)

As a member, what would you like **BLACK CAT ENGLISH CLUB** to offer:

❑ Member gathering/ party ❑ English class with native teacher ❑ English competition
❑ Newsletter ❑ Online sharing ❑ Book fair
❑ Book discount ❑ Others (please specify: ____________________)

Other suggestions to **BLACK CAT ENGLISH CLUB**:

____

Please sign here: ____________________

(Date: ____________________)